❦ DESCEND ❦

SKYE MALONE

Descend
Book two of the Awakened Fate series

Copyright © 2014 by Skye Malone

Published by Wildflower Isle | P.O. Box 17804, Urbana, IL 61803

ISBN: 1-940617-11-1
ISBN-13: 978-1-940617-11-4

Library of Congress Control Number: 2014906857

Cover design by Karri Klawiter
www.artbykarri.com

PRONUNCIATION GUIDE

Aveluria (av-eh-LUR-ee-uh)

Dehaian (deh-HYE-an)

Driecara (dree-eh-CAR-uh)

Fejeria (feh-JER-ee-uh)

Greliaran (greh-lee-AR-an)

Ina (EE-na)

Inasaria (ee-na-SAR-ee-uh)

Jirral (jur-AHL)

Kirzan (KUR-zahn)

Lycera (ly-SER-uh)

Neiphiandine (ney-fee-AN-deen)

Niall (nee-AHL)

Nialloran (nee-ah-LOR-en)

Nyciena (ny-SEE-en-uh)

Ociras (oh-SHE-rahs)

Renekialen (ren-eh-kee-AHL-en)

Ryaira (ry-AIR-uh)

Sieranchine (see-EHR-an-cheen)

Siracha (seer-AH-cha)

Sylphaen (sil-FAY-en)

Teariad (tee-AR-ee-ad)

Torvias (TOR-vee-ahs)

Velior (VEH-lee-or)

Yvaria (ih-VAR-ee-uh)

Zekerian (zeh-KEHR-ee-en)

PROLOGUE

NOAH

Waves rolled into the shore, their white-noise rush undercutting the cries of the seagulls overhead. The afternoon sun glinted on the water, turning the ocean into a rippling fabric of light.

Chloe was gone.

No fins broke the water's surface, no scales flashed above the waves. The dehaians had disappeared as though they'd never come to Santa Lucina at all.

And if what they'd said was right, there was every chance that, in Chloe's case at least, she wouldn't be back for a very long time.

Not with the strength of those drugs in her system.

I turned from the water. The thought hurt, twisting in my chest in a way I'd never experienced before, and I shook my head, trying to drive it away. She was safer out there, safer with her own kind. I hated it, but it was true. Her life was in danger here. Letting her go was the best thing I could do for her.

No matter how hard it was to make myself believe the words.

I reached the shore, my clothes dripping and my sandals squelching under my feet. Shifting my shoulders against the cold fabric clinging to my skin, I glanced back at the ocean, wondering how far away and how deep she was now.

"Well, aren't you just a picture?"

I turned, tensing as much from surprise as to keep my skin from changing. The greliaran defenses were hard to control, and the last thing I needed was some tourist running off with stories of meeting a monster with fire in his skin on the Santa Lucina shore.

My uncle Richard came down the wooden stairs from the top of the bluffs.

"What are you doing here?" I asked warily.

"Your dad called. Asked us to keep an eye on the place while you all were at the cabin." Richard looked me up and down, disgust twitching his lip. "You've got a lot of nerve."

I didn't respond.

"Letting her go," he continued. "Keeping any of them alive."

"She's gone now. She can't come back. It doesn't matter."

His mouth curved, though only the most naïve would've called the expression a smile.

"You better hope not," he replied. "I'd hate to have to kill her for you."

1

CHLOE

I kicked hard in the water, trying to keep up with the dehaians in front of me.

"You doing alright?" Zeke called from a short distance ahead.

I didn't respond. I wasn't, really. Everything was new now. The wide, partially translucent fin that had replaced my feet. The iridescent scales that ran down the long tail that my legs had become and up over my chest like some sort of bizarre evening gown. The skin of my arms and shoulders glistened, as if they were covered in gold dust. Instincts I hadn't known I possessed had kept me moving with the others for the past hour, though every time I started to think about what I was doing, I floundered.

Though that wasn't the real problem.

I'd left everything back on the shore. Friends, family, everything I'd known.

And Noah.

I drew a breath, trying to push away the ache that the thought caused, though fear just followed on its heels. Crazy men had injected me with some kind of drug that had forced me into the dehaians' underwater form, making it impossible to survive outside the ocean. I could barely breathe normal air and rising above the water's surface made my skin hurt like I had the world's worst sunburn. Half my body was locked in a permanent tail now, and changing back seemed utterly beyond me.

But the drug had to wear off eventually, I reminded myself. And if willpower had anything to do with that timeframe, I'd have the chemicals out of my system within the hour.

I pushed myself to swim faster. I'd come back to Santa Lucina. I'd see Noah again. Drugs and fins and total psychos wouldn't stop that.

Zeke dropped back to match my pace. "Chloe?"

"I'm fine."

He didn't seem to believe me, if his hesitant expression was any sign.

"We can slow down if you want?"

I was silent. I could tell by the way the others shot ahead every so often that they were already moving at a much slower pace than they ever would normally.

His mouth tightened. "Hey," he called to the men.

"It's fine," I insisted, keeping my voice low as they looked back.

"That stuff the Sylphaen gave you might hurt you if you

push too hard," he replied, his voice as quiet as mine. "Besides, it's a pretty decent trip across Yvaria to Nyciena. Even if we don't stop, we won't make it there till long past midnight anyway."

I grimaced. Truth be told, I was tired. I'd never been swimming before in my life, and even though Noah had told me dehaians were strong, obviously I wasn't. At least, not anything like them. I wanted to get back to the doctors Zeke said could help me, but the pace was starting to make my muscles hurt.

"Okay," I agreed reluctantly.

Niall turned back toward us. Zeke had introduced him as his older brother and with his black hair, silver-dusted skin, and scales only a few shades lighter than Zeke's own, he certainly looked like it. As he swam closer, he smiled at me, his sapphire eyes glinting with a roguish touch that probably melted hearts back where he was from.

"Everything alright?" he asked.

"Let's camp here," Zeke said. "Pick back up tomorrow."

Niall glanced from me to Zeke, and then he shrugged. "Yeah, okay." He looked back to the others. "Guys. Find a spot to set up camp."

The dehaians altered course, diving down to the seafloor several dozen yards below us. I had no idea how deep we were – or how we were surviving in whatever pressure there was at this depth, for that matter – but we'd been coasting just above the bottom of the ocean for quite some time. I knew I shouldn't have been able to see it; this far down, even the ghost of the sandy terrain below should have been invisible. But I was also fairly certain that, similar to the others, my eyes were glowing and somehow amplifying even the tiniest traces of light, compensating for darkness that otherwise would've left me blind.

At a spot like any other on the mostly featureless seafloor, the dehaians stopped, and one of them shrugged off the bag that was slung crosswise over his bare chest. Tools unlike anything I'd seen emerged from the bag, tugged out by the man and handed around to the others, who took off without a word. As I came closer, one of them circled the campsite, a stone in his hand with glowing white runes carved into its surface.

The sand seemed to shiver, and then a curtain of tiny bubbles rose from the seafloor, forming a dome over us all.

I looked to Zeke.

"Refractive veil," he explained. "Or just a veil for short. Bends light and sound in a way that renders us pretty much invisible to anything passing by."

My brow furrowed. We were at the bottom of the ocean, God knew how far from the coast. What could see us?

He read the question in my eyes. "You know, deep sea explorers. Dangerous fish."

"Crazy people," Niall added.

I swallowed. Right. Of course.

A flicker caught my eye and I turned. Blue flames rose from

a spot on the sand, snapping and twisting like a campfire but without the wood. A dehaian leaned away from the impossible fire, another weird stone device in his hand and a satisfied look on his face.

"Water-torches," Zeke said. "When we're not moving as much, we get colder, and they..."

He trailed off as I looked back at him again.

"There's a lot to explain," he finished. "A lot that's different down here."

I gave a vague nod, my gaze slipping back to the campsite. Heat came off of the fire, warming the water that had just started to feel cold around me. Over our heads, the veil reflected the glow and turned the dark water to pale twilight. With the agility of eels, the other dehaians darted around the camp, clearing away the larger rocks and shells amid the gray sand or setting up glowing blue stones by the base of the veil.

Different wasn't the half of it.

"Come on," Zeke said.

I followed him. On the seafloor, he sank down next to the flames, curling his tail beneath him. I attempted to do the same, succeeding only in toppling sideways. Pushing back upright, I braced myself with one arm, using the other to shove the fin that had been my feet out of the way. Blushing with embarrassment, I glanced to the others, but none of them were looking my direction.

A frustrated sigh escaped me. I missed my legs. At least I knew how to operate those without falling over.

"Hey Zeke," Niall said into the awkward silence. "You remember that time I got stuck in the fejeria?"

Zeke chuckled. "I remember the way you were yelling for someone to get you out of there."

Niall grinned. "There's these plants, right?" he said to me. "They grow in Nyciena and we use them kind of like doors. Well, when you want, you can make them seal up so people can't get inside your place. It's like a security feature. So, I'd snuck out to see this girl – what was her name again?" he asked Zeke.

"Taliana, the Lyceran ambassador's daughter. He tried to use your visit as a bargaining chip with Dad."

"Oh yeah. Well, anyway," Niall continued to me, "I'd snuck out and I thought I could get back in time. But as I was coming inside, someone set the security code and..." he laughed, "the damn things sealed up right around me. Pinned me good and tight, smack in the center of the doorframe."

"I think Dad wanted to leave you," Zeke added. "Teach you a lesson or something."

"Yeah, wouldn't that've looked good? Though he *did* end up sending me to the west garrison for six months as punishment." Niall glanced back at me, grinning. "But then, that's nothing like the time Zeke here–"

"Hey, tell your own stories," Zeke interjected.

"Why?" Niall protested innocently. "Yours are so much fun."

A smile tugged at my lip as Zeke glared at him.

"I could tell her about the time Ren threw a tantrum and got his spikes stuck in the nursery wall," Niall offered.

"Oh, come on. That's not fair. He was six."

Niall shrugged. "Still funny."

Zeke shook his head, though he couldn't quite hide his amusement as well.

I glanced between them, grateful for how they were trying to make me feel better, no matter how strange this all still seemed. I was breathing water, as far as I could tell, though it felt as effortless as taking in air. Scales were my only covering now, running the length of my tail and continuing up over my chest to taper away near my shoulders – although from what I could see, my back was still just skin. The guys around me didn't even have that, however. Their scales ended at their waists, and their chests were bare. It had felt awkward at first, being surrounded by a dozen well-built, essentially shirtless guys, but over the hours, my awareness of their appearance and mine had begun to disappear.

Which was also strange. I'd expected this dehaian thing to seem more alien. It made me feel ungainly, yes. But it was also inexplicably natural.

And that was more disturbing than anything.

Overhead, one of the dehaians swam back through the veil surrounding the campsite, and the others glanced up. In his hand, he held a ring attached to a rope of seaweed, and multiple fish on hooks dangled from it.

"Nice," Niall commented at the sight.

The man pulled up by the ocean floor. With fast motions, he removed the fish from the hooks and then cleaned them with a small knife. Reaching back into his bag, he drew out a brown bowl and quickly set to cutting the fish apart, trapping the pieces in the bowl as he went.

Zeke smiled at me as the man brought the fish over to us. "You ever had…" He glanced to Niall. "What do they call it again?"

"Sushi. Or sashimi. That's the one without the rice."

"Right. That?"

I shook my head. Like water, pictures of the ocean, and the color blue, sushi had been on my parents' list of things they'd get furious about if I came near.

"Okay, well, this is basically the same thing. Minus the rice."

I nodded, though I couldn't keep the dubious expression from my face. I waited as Zeke and Niall drew pieces out with their fingers, and then I did the same. Trying not to wince at the odd feeling of the fish, I lifted it up and took a cautious bite.

It tasted amazing.

I looked to Zeke.

He grinned. "You–"

Niall made a tense noise, cutting him off as the glowing stones by the base of the veil went red. Brow furrowing, I followed his gaze upward.

From the gloom above the campsite, a dozen dehaians emerged. Straps crisscrossed their chests, with stone knives in slots along both bands, and belts with long swords encircled their waists. Vicious scars puckered their skin and scales, and one wore an eye patch beneath his fiery hair. I swallowed at the sight of them, my heart pounding.

In silence, we watched them swim past, and it wasn't till they disappeared into the shadows again that I remembered to breathe.

"Mercenaries?" Zeke said, his quiet voice incredulous. "What the hell are they doing east of the Prijoran Zone?"

Niall shook his head, still studying the direction in which the dehaians had gone.

Another moment crept by and then Zeke let out a breath. "Weird," he commented idly.

Niall glanced to him, meeting his gaze for a moment. "Yeah, no kidding," he said, his tone the same.

They went back to eating.

I looked between them, knowing what they were trying to do.

"Are we in danger?" I asked, keeping my voice down.

Niall shook his head dismissively.

I watched Zeke.

He twitched his head toward the dehaians around us. "These guys… well, let's just say they're *very* good fighters."

"And we're not half-bad either," Niall added between bites of fish.

Zeke scoffed at his brother, and then gave me a smile. "We'll be fine. It's just unusual for Vetorians to be around

11

here. But they won't mess with us."

"Because they didn't even see us," Niall pointed out.

"And we'll be home tomorrow."

I nodded, trying to take the reassurances at face value. Zeke had said the dehaians with us were guards, though he'd been vague on what exactly it was they typically guarded. They didn't have any weapons that I could see – besides their spikes, anyway – and their only uniform seemed to consist of a black armband with a strange, mountain-like symbol stitched in glistening blue thread on the side. But regardless, the men did appear able to take care of themselves; there wasn't a one of them whose muscles weren't practically chiseled onto their torsos. For that matter, Zeke and Niall were making a good show of being unconcerned too, and hadn't glanced at the water overhead again.

Which was nice. Those guys had still looked terrifying, though.

I swallowed hard and picked up another piece of fish, trying to force my appetite to return. I didn't know what I'd expected upon coming down here, though safety from people who might want to hurt me had probably been on the list.

And maybe that could still be the case. Maybe once we reached Zeke and Niall's home, I'd finally stand a chance of being someplace mercenaries and Sylphaen and God knew what else couldn't find me.

At least, I hoped.

∾ 2 ∾

ZEKE

"So what do you think those mercenaries *were* doing here?" Niall asked me quietly. "The border patrols should have stopped them ages ago."

I didn't answer, watching Chloe while the guards swam around us, getting ready to leave. Curled on the sand, she slept, the blue-white light of the fire flickering against the iridescent sheen of her cream-toned scales. Currents twisted through her hair, which was redder than it had seemed on land, and occasionally the gold-dusted skin of her brow furrowed, as though she was fighting something in her dreams.

And all around her, a faint hum quivered through the water, like the ocean was ever-so-slightly electrified.

Niall said something, and I blinked. "What?"

His lip twitched. "I said the change looks good on her. Or wouldn't you agree?"

I glanced back at her. "Uh, yeah, I guess."

"You *guess?*" He looked from me to Chloe and then scoffed. "You feeling alright?"

"Fine."

"Uh-huh."

I gave him an irritated look. "What?"

"Oh, nothing. But if you're not going to make a move on her, you better be sure I will."

"No, I–"

I cut off the hurried response, uncertain what I'd planned to say. But Niall just paused.

"Wait," he said. "You're not..."

"Not what?" I asked when he trailed off.

Niall cleared his throat. "You're not like actually *falling* for her, are you?"

"Huh?"

He paused, a weird look on his face, and then he suddenly let out an incredulous chuckle. "Well, I... damn that's, um..."

"That's what?" I demanded. "Niall, give me a break. I barely know the girl."

"Yeah, and yet you wanted all these guys to come to Santa Lucina to rescue her."

"You know it wasn't like that."

His amusement grew. "Uh-huh."

"Oh for pity's sake, Niall. Do you feel the water around us? Feel how it's different with her in it?"

"It's different, huh?"

"I will kick your ass, you keep this up."

Amusement still tweaked his expression, but it lessened. "Okay, the water." He glanced around. "It's… I mean…" His brow furrowed.

"See what I'm talking about?"

"Are you sure there's not just a storm topside or something? I know you said strange things happened with the water when you saw her before, but maybe…"

"You ever felt a storm do this?"

"No," he allowed. "But… come on. She can't really be—"

"It's happened every time I've seen her. Something similar, anyway. And the second she leaves the water, it stops."

I looked back at Chloe. She gave a soft cry in her sleep and I hesitated, wondering if I should go wake her. But after a moment, she seemed to calm down.

"Maybe it was a coincidence," Niall tried.

I met the words with a flat look. "*Every* time? And that's not the only thing. The second time I saw her, she was attacked. By water. Black, frigid water like you'd find deeper than Nyciena, but off the Santa Lucina coast."

He paused. "Okay, now you're just making stuff up."

I shook my head.

Niall's brow drew down and he looked away. My gaze returned to Chloe.

She seemed to be sleeping better now. And the strange feeling in the water remained. It wasn't quite the same as when I'd first seen her – then, it'd been unmistakable for miles around. Now, it was fainter. Almost diluted, though that made little sense. It seemed like something was dampening it, keeping it from being as... *clear*... in the water as it had been before, to the point where if, like Niall, I hadn't been waiting for it, I might've missed the feeling.

I scowled. Maybe the difference was caused by the drug the Sylphaen had given her. Or something else I wasn't aware of. Before Chloe had come along, I'd never felt anything like this. And now, anything was possible, since what she was doing *shouldn't* have been.

And she didn't even seem to know it was happening.

"So what do you want to tell Dad when we get home?" Niall asked. "Assuming he agrees to talk to us, I mean."

I turned back to him. "The truth?" I hazarded.

"No, seriously."

"We have to tell him about the Sylphaen. And the best chance we have of keeping her safe from them means she stays nearby."

"She doesn't have any family at all down here?"

"None she seems to know of. She said she grew up on land. She wasn't even aware dehaians existed until I told her."

"Wow." Niall watched her a moment and then sighed. "Even so, he'll want to put out a search. See if she has relatives to take her in. You know, for propriety's sake."

I grimaced. Dad and propriety. With kids like us, minus Ren anyway, I knew he would insist on finding her family and making certain who she was. Scandals were the last thing he needed.

Though that didn't stop it from being annoying.

"If he puts out word that she's in Nyciena, the Sylphaen might hear," I argued. "He'll understand keeping it quiet."

"That's *if* he believes the Sylphaen are real."

I gave Niall an exasperated glance.

"What?" he protested. "I'm just saying, he's not the most believing kind."

"So help me convince him."

Niall looked at me tiredly. "Of course I will." He paused. "Maybe if we got Ren to believe us, this'd go better."

"He's worse than Dad."

"And Dad knows that. If Ren believes us, Dad will listen, no questions asked."

I sighed. That, at least, was true. It wasn't the way I wanted to go about this, though – Ren was stubborn as hell, and if he got it in his head we were lying, it'd be almost impossible to change his mind. But Niall was still right. If we could convince him, things with Dad would go much more smoothly.

Hopefully, anyway. Kindness and sympathy weren't exactly Dad's strong suits.

"So who do you think she is, really?" Niall asked, watching Chloe again. "Or, you know... what."

I shook my head. "No idea."

"Have you told her about us?"

I paused, and then shook my head again.

His amusement returned. "Seriously? You didn't even *try* playing that—"

"I'm not chasing her, Niall."

He eyed me for a moment, still appearing amused. "If you say so."

I scowled, looking back at Chloe. It wasn't like that, whatever Niall thought. I hadn't said anything about my family because there hadn't been time, and because there'd been bigger issues at hand. Issues like powerful and dangerous drugs. Like electrified, possessed water.

Like the fact that nearly every time I'd seen the girl, a psychotic cult had been trying to kill her.

"How about we see if the guards have figured out the best way back yet, now that the Vetorians are around?" I suggested, unable to keep the annoyance from my voice. "You know, get home before they spot us?"

He grinned. "Okay," he agreed, a touch indulgently. "If you'd rather talk about that than–"

"Niall."

He laughed.

I shook my head in exasperation. I knew him. He wasn't going to let up on this. Not when there was the chance of some entertainment at my expense – no matter *how* wrong he was about the whole thing. Chloe was intriguing, yes, but because of the mystery surrounding what she did and the question of why the Sylphaen were after her. And she was attractive as well. She'd been beautiful before this and the change looked amazing on her now. I wasn't blind.

But none of that was the point. Chloe wasn't just another

girl to pursue. Even in the incredibly short time I'd known her, that'd become clear. With Chloe, it was... more complicated. She hadn't grown up dehaian and she wasn't like us. Not really. She didn't know about our world, about her new form, about any of it. And to ignore all that just to get her into bed with me... I couldn't. The thought was vaguely nauseating, since it'd feel too much like manipulating her and taking advantage of how confusing this all was for her right now.

And no matter what Ren or others in Nyciena thought, taking advantage of girls had *never* been my style.

Besides, I'd seen her with that other boy. The human, in the surf moments after her body transformed for the first time. She hadn't wanted to leave him. And yes, *if* I'd cared to chase her, that would've just been a challenge to overcome.

But it wasn't like that. Not this time.

Chloe was different.

3

NOAH

The front door slammed.

Sitting on the couch, I didn't look up. Around the living room, my four behemoth cousins leaned on the walls with their overly muscled arms crossed in front of them, looking for all the world like the near-identical, sadistic meatheads that they were. Watching me and the ocean beyond our windows alike, they made no secret of their disgust for me, or their anticipation for what they'd try if the dehaians returned.

"Noah?" my dad called.

"In here, Peter," Richard replied.

Silence followed the words, and then I heard his footsteps coming down the hall.

Dad walked around the corner, taking in the five of them and me seated in the middle.

"Are you alright?" he asked me.

"He's fine," Richard answered before I could speak. "Except for having a fling with a scum-sucker, that is."

Dad paused. "What happened?"

"Your son—"

"I asked Noah."

Richard snorted, derision in his dark brown eyes, and then he gestured for me to go ahead.

"Nothing," I said, not wanting to get into it in front of the others. "She's gone."

Dad regarded me for a moment.

"He let her go, he means," Richard inserted. "Kissed her goodbye and let her swim away." He rounded on Dad. "This is what I've been warning you about. You, and the way you raise these boys. You can't keep—"

"This isn't the time, Richard," Dad countered.

His brother scoffed. "You called me, remember? Even you can see how dangerous this is. That *thing* was staying with your family, for pity's sake! And now you've got scale-skins breaking into your house. What's next?" He shook his head. "What's it going to take, Peter? Are you really going to risk your sons, just to hang onto your pathetic principles?"

Dad paused and then looked over at him, and I could see his anger in the tense muscles of his face.

"I said this wasn't the time," he repeated. "I called you here, yes." His gaze flicked to me. "And you'll stay. Keep an eye out for them, in case they come back. But you will leave my sons to me, understand?"

Richard's lip twitched with disgust, but he just shook his head. "Fine. You let your pretty boys stay weak. And my sons and I will hold up the *true* family heritage and keep things safe. Just like always."

He motioned to his sons and then headed for the hallway. Shrugging away from the walls, my cousins smirked at me as they followed him out of the room.

Their footsteps thudded on the steps as they went upstairs.

A breath left me. "Dad, you can't–"

He held up a hand, silencing me with his eyes on the ceiling.

I grimaced. They'd hear us if we talked, even all the way in the guest rooms. Greliaran hearing could be a bitch sometimes.

And that didn't bring into it the other senses we had.

Doors closed above us. I could feel them moving across the rooms, heading for the windows to keep watch and not even bothering to hide their presences from me anymore.

I looked back at Dad.

He switched on the stereo, letting the white noise babble of a local radio station cut through the quiet.

"Diane told me they shot you and Maddox," he said, keeping his voice low.

My words faltered.

"What the hell were you *thinking*, Noah?"

"Dad, I–"

He crossed the room and put his arms around me. I blinked, taken back by the gesture.

Releasing a breath, he pushed me away again. "What happened?"

I struggled for words, still floundering with shock. "I-I went after Chloe, and while I was gone they came to the cabin."

"They knew about us?"

A short scoff escaped me, not quite a laugh since nothing was funny. "Dad, you sent one of them through a window and nearly put the other through the wall. I think they figured out we weren't human."

He gave me a dark look and my sarcasm died.

"And then you brought her here."

"I had to. They'd injected her with something. It was killing her. Forcing her to change into one of them even though she wasn't in the water. If I hadn't gotten her to the ocean…"

Dad sighed, turning away and pacing across the room. "Will she come back?"

I paused. "The other ones said she couldn't. Not till that drug was gone."

"Other ones?"

The grimace tried to return. "Dehaians. They met us on the beach. I think they were looking for her."

He ran a hand over his hair. "Noah…"

"I didn't know they'd be there! I…"

Frustrated, I looked down, not sure what I was attempting to say. I'd been trying to save her life. I couldn't let her die.

A breath escaped me. She'd just been Baylie's friend. The beautiful, kind-of-shy girl who avoided me when I visited Kansas on holidays, though I'd never been able to figure out why. I'd always hoped to talk to her, and when she'd finally come to Santa Lucina and I had the chance…

My fists curled against the memory of my last moments with her. Of kissing her and feeling her against me. I'd wanted to do that for weeks, ever since that first night on the beach. She'd looked amazing by the water, silhouetted by the moonlight, and everything about her fascinated me. I'd held back, though, thinking what I was would make things difficult. Thinking she was human.

I'd never expected this.

"You can't let her come back here," Dad said, turning to me. "Understand?"

I looked up at him. His face hardened at my expression.

"I mean it," he said. "This is for her sake as much as yours."

"Well, if you wouldn't let Uncle Richard and his–"

"They stay." He paused. "Those dehaian bastards *shot* you and Maddox. Next time, maybe they'll keep shooting till you won't be able to recover from the wounds. I'm not going to take that chance."

"But Dad, Chloe isn't–"

"She's a danger to us. And we're a danger to her. This isn't going to work, Noah." He sighed, sympathy tingeing his gaze. "I know you like her, son. She seems like a nice girl. But she's dehaian, and right now…" He glanced to the upper floor briefly. "I'll talk to Richard. Make sure the boys understand she's not to be harmed. But I'm not risking you, which means your uncle and your cousins *will* stay, at least for now. And if she does come back…" He shook his head. "I want you to make her leave again, for good this time. No matter what it takes."

I stared at him. "Dad…"

"I mean it, Noah."

A breath left me. Protests formed and died at the look in his eyes.

Dumbstruck, I managed a nod.

Echoing the motion more firmly, he regarded me a moment longer and then turned away, switching off the stereo. Taking out his cell, he climbed the short steps from the sunken living room and headed out through the back door. I heard him talking to Diane on the phone as he walked across the yard.

I closed my eyes. Short of Chloe being dead, I didn't know how this could have gone much worse. And that wasn't to say she wouldn't be. Not with my cousins around.

Exhaling sharply, I turned to the windows and the brilliant sunset beyond. Dad didn't know those guys like I did. They'd always managed to hide how they were from him, and in any case he thought Richard controlled them.

Instead of just egging them on.

My arm rested against the glass, though I really just wanted to break it. My brother and I, my dad, we all fought what we were. What our instincts demanded we do. We all felt the cravings – the way our greliaran sides whispered of the need to kill dehaians, and of the incredible rush from absorbing their magic that would follow – but Dad had taught us to be more than that. More than bloodthirsty monsters created by old wizards to defend against fish people. More than weird mash-ups of human and dehaian traits that left us something wildly different than both.

But my cousins weren't.

And that was what it all came down to in the end. My cousins gloried in being greliaran. Loved the strength, the power. They were salivating at the prospect of killing a dehaian, and after a lifetime of never seeing a single one…

They'd hunt her. For as long as they thought she'd come back here, they'd be watching day and night, waiting for the chance to rip her apart.

Anger rose. I wouldn't let them hurt her, though. Whether the rest of the stories my grandfather had told about her kind were true, I still wouldn't. It didn't matter. She wasn't like the dehaians he'd described – the sadistic, pleasure-seeking, soulless creatures who charmed innocent people into loving them and then let them die – and I wasn't a murderer. I wouldn't let my cousins become ones either. Not with her.

No matter what it took.

4

CHLOE

I opened my eyes to nothing but endless blue in front of me and, despite my nightmares about the Sylphaen and the worries of the evening before, I couldn't help but smile.

It was just like my dreams.

Drawing a deep breath, I pushed away from the sand. The fire still flickered several yards away, and Zeke and Niall sat near it. All the other dehaians were likewise up, making me wonder how long I'd been sleeping while they all got ready to go.

Niall laughed at something and Zeke looked away, irritation on his face.

He caught sight of me.

"Hey there," he said, his annoyance disappearing.

Niall glanced over. "Morning."

"Hi," I said, blushing with embarrassment. "Sorry I slept so late."

Zeke shook his head. "You didn't."

I smiled, grateful for the way he kept trying to make things okay. "Are we going soon?"

"Yeah." He glanced to Niall. "We were just talking about how maybe you could stay with us for a while, once we get back to Nyciena."

I paused. "That'd be nice. If there's room, I mean. I don't want to impose."

Niall chuckled. "Oh, there'll be room."

Zeke gave his brother a brief glare, and then turned a reassuring look on me. "It'll be fine."

"Thank you."

He smiled.

One of the dehaians came over and said something to Niall.

"Okay," he replied. He glanced to us. "Ready to head out?"

Zeke nodded and kicked up from the sand easily, and after a bit of floundering, I managed to leave the ground as well. The veil around the campsite fell away, disappearing back into the seafloor as though it'd never been, while the fire did the same.

And in only a moment, nothing remained to show we'd been there.

"Cool, huh?" Niall commented when he noticed me watching the space where the fire had burned. "Wait till you see Nyciena."

I smiled, though the comment sent a flutter of trepidation

through me. Everything here had me gawking enough.

Nyciena would probably be overwhelming.

The guards set off and I followed with Zeke and Niall joining me on either side. It was easier to keep up with them today, and as the hours continued on, I didn't have to slow down once. Past underwater valleys and hills we swam, weaving our way along a path the guards seemed to know without question.

And gradually, a realization spread over me.

I was aware of the hills and valleys before I saw them.

My brow furrowed. The gloom beyond us looked impenetrable, and yet, if I focused, I knew there was a valley inside it. Likewise, an array of hills lay to our right, with a smattering of caves midway up on this side, though their other side was a mystery.

I knew it all. I just couldn't see any of it.

"You okay?" Zeke asked.

I blinked and turned to him. "I, um... is there a valley ahead of us? I mean... can you, like, feel that it's there?"

He nodded. "Yeah."

I stared at him.

Sympathy touched his face. "It's just how we are, Chloe. It's fine. You probably just didn't notice yesterday because you're still adjusting to all this."

"But how is that even possible?"

He shrugged. "Combination of hearing, sight, smell... your skin is pretty sensitive too. That's part of why air burns if you're above water and you don't change it a bit. But yeah, all of that. Our sight's really good, but it's not the only way we navigate."

I looked down as the valley I'd felt emerged from the gloom.

"It'll get easier," Zeke assured me. "Just give it time."

I nodded, hoping he was right.

We swam onward, the miles passing below us in the form of small plains, rolling hills, and little valleys. Invisible in the water far overhead, a pod of whales drifted by, their cries barely reaching my ears.

A sense of blackness and cold prickled my skin. I looked down as the plains gave way to a canyon so deep, I couldn't feel its end.

I shivered, suddenly feeling so tiny as we continued over the trench.

"Nyciena ahead," Niall commented.

I pulled my gaze from the valley, my eyes searching the featureless water and seeing nothing.

And then I blinked. I could feel it, past the gloom, rising up from the depths of the canyon.

It felt like a mountain.

One of the guards slowed and lifted his hand, wordlessly signaling the rest. My brow furrowed as Zeke and Niall pulled up.

"Someone's coming," Zeke explained quietly.

I swallowed.

Six dehaians swam toward us from the murk, and all of them were armed with objects that looked remarkably like guns.

"What the hell?" Zeke protested at the sight.

"Nice to see you too, Zeke," one commented as he came closer.

I looked between them. With the same black hair and gunmetal scales as Zeke, the man could easily have been related to him and Niall, although in Zeke's case the guy seemed at least ten years older. Unlike the two brothers, however, his face was stern, with a jaw that appeared made of granite and blue eyes that had probably never seen anything they deemed worthy of a laugh. His bearing was likewise firm, as if everything his gaze touched belonged to him – with the expectation that it had dare not present a problem. As his eyes scanned over me, I tensed, suddenly uncomfortable at being in what he obviously considered *his* ocean.

"What's with the welcoming party, Ren?" Niall asked, his tone lighter, though it sounded forced. "There a problem?"

The man ignored him. "Is this her?"

"Is this who?" Niall asked. "We're just–"

"Is this her?" the man repeated, his tone hardening.

Zeke hesitated. "Chloe," he said to me, his head turning my way though his eyes never left the other man. "Meet my brother, Ren."

Annoyance twitched Ren's face. "You should have cleared bringing her here with me," he said, tucking his weapon into a slot on his belt.

"There wasn't time," Zeke replied. "She needs medical attention."

Ren looked me over again. "Medical attention?"

"Yes. The Sylphaen gave her a drug. We need the doctors to look at her."

"She seems fine."

Zeke stared at him. "They gave her a *drug*. As in, they injected her with it? She needs help, Ren. Trust me."

I tried not to shift position in the water, hating the way Ren kept eyeing me like he wasn't sure if I was a person or an insect.

"And did you *see* these Sylphaen?" Ren asked.

Zeke looked incredulous. "I told you I did when I called from the relay station."

"Did you see them give her this drug?"

"I – no, but I saw what it did to her."

Ren's mouth tightened.

"These guys are real, Ren," Niall said.

"You saw them?"

Niall faltered. "Well, no, but I–"

"So we have nothing but her word that there is anything in her system requiring attention. And nothing but yours, Zeke, that the people in question were not simply pretending to be members of a cult that has been dead for a hundred years." He looked at his brother tiredly. "I told you to come back to Nyciena and let us handle things. Matters like this are infinitely more complicated now, given the current situation."

"Current situation?" Zeke repeated. "What are you–"

"Since you've been gone, we've had a dozen raids on the Prijoran border, outcasts have been spotted hiding near the capital, and our scouts have received whispers that the Vetorian mercenaries are joining forces, with an eye toward expanding their territory into our own. And now she shows up as a damsel in distress – with an unverifiable story, no less – desperately in need of help from arguably one of the least... disciplined... among us. Help which involves bringing her straight past our defenses. How convenient."

Zeke's jaw worked angrily. "She's not a spy. I've seen what they did to–"

"Take her to the northwest border outpost," Ren interrupted, glancing to the men behind him. "And put her under guard. We'll send a doctor there."

Zeke drew in front of them. "No, the Sylphaen are still after her. She won't be safe there."

"Oh, of course not. I'm sure she claims she *must* be taken directly here."

"No, *I'm* the one who's taking her here. If you'd get out of our way, that is."

Ren's condescension deepened. "I'm not endangering the city so you can impress your latest piece of ass with affectations of chivalry, brother."

My brow climbed.

Zeke's face flushed red, and I couldn't tell if it was from

embarrassment or outrage. "Fuck off, Ren," he growled. "I'm bringing her to see Dad."

"No, you–"

Niall swam between them quickly as Zeke started forward. "Hey! Hey now. Zeke, calm down." He held up his hands. "Look, Ren. We've got her under guard. You want her blind-folded too? We can do that. But just in *case* this is true, you don't want the trouble of her dying while we wait for a doctor to get all the way out to the northwest border, right?"

Ren gave him an exasperated look. Niall's eyebrow rose questioningly.

"Really, Ren," he pressed. "Spy or not, you think Dad wants to deal with that?"

The man studied him for a moment, and then his cold gaze slid over to me. My skin crawled at the derision in his eyes.

"Blindfolded, then," Ren agreed. "And tied. Armed guards as well, and you two keep away from her."

Alarmed, I looked between them all, my heart pounding.

"No!" Zeke snapped. "Ren, you don't have to–"

"Or I send her to the outpost. Which do you prefer?"

"I'll stay with her," Niall interjected before Zeke could answer. "Okay? In case Zeke's not wrong. We don't want to cause problems, right? Let's just bring her to see Dad and let him decide what to do."

Ren regarded his brother, and then jerked his chin at the guards. They swam forward, four of them taking aim at me with the weapons in their hands while the fifth pulled a black hood and a pair of long, metal manacles from the bag on his shoulder.

Adrenaline surged through me at the sight, bringing back a rush of panic like I'd felt when the Sylphaen had trapped me in an ambulance the day before. Eyes wide, I retreated, my skin stinging as spikes pushed from my arms.

"Ren, she's not a criminal!" Zeke protested, attempting to get between me and the guards. They grabbed him, keeping him from moving farther, and Zeke shoved at them. "You can't–"

"Hey!" Niall cut in, kicking briefly and then pulling up near me in the water. "Zeke, Chloe, everybody. Calm down."

He reached out and touched my arm.

I flinched, the spikes growing longer.

"Hey," he repeated. "We'll be right here, okay? No one's going to shoot. You're safe. Ren, for pity's sake, she's a girl, not a monster. Have them put the weapons down."

"No."

Niall made an aggravated noise. "Fine then. Zeke? *One* of you help me here."

Blocked by three guards between us, Zeke gave a quick look to Niall, and then followed the deliberate twitch of his brother's gaze toward me.

He caught sight of my arms.

"Chloe, listen to me." Zeke drew a breath, obviously working to calm down. "Just keep the spikes in. Don't let them out so

35

the manacles won't hurt you, okay? And stay with Niall."

The guards swam closer.

"Breathe," Niall said, putting a hand to my upper arm. "Both of you. It's only for a few minutes. It'll be fine."

Holding the manacles, the guard pulled up near me. I stared at him.

"Let the spikes retract, Chloe," Niall urged, his other hand moving to my shoulder. "We're right here. They won't shoot you. Ren's just being a jerk, okay? He's good at that. But no one's shooting anyone today. You're fine."

I looked to Niall. He nodded reassuringly, letting me go. I took a breath and slowly, the spikes crept into my skin.

The guard snapped the manacles on my forearms the moment they disappeared. I gasped, tensing all over again. The spikes tried to return, and ran into the metal instead.

A jolt of electricity shot through me at the contact and I cried out in pain.

Zeke darted toward me, only to be stopped by the guards.

"No, no, no," Niall interjected, his grip returning to my shoulder. "Spikes back, okay? It's just going to hurt more if you don't stop them. Right, Zeke?"

Seeming as if he was fighting not to explode, Zeke tugged away from the guards. Gasping, I met his eyes.

He nodded tensely. "It's just for a minute. We'll be right here."

The guard yanked the hood over my head, and then clipped something to its side.

Numbness rushed through me, deadening everything but the feeling of Niall's hands on the skin of my back and arms. I choked, and then shrieked again as a stronger burst of electricity jolted me from my spikes contacting the shackles.

Niall's grip vanished sharply and then returned. "Breathe," he urged, his voice duller from the force of whatever the thing on the hood had done. "You can breathe. Just stay calm."

Trembling, I tried to do as he said.

He swam forward, bringing me with him.

I couldn't feel the water. Not like I had. Gel moved over my face, my arms and tail, its touch neither hot nor cold. The viscous muck slid in through my nose and mouth with each breath, and it took everything I had to believe that I wouldn't suffocate. Niall's warm hands gripped me, his touch the only thing still keeping me grounded when all my senses screamed that something was horribly wrong.

"Almost there," Niall said, his words warped and muffled.

Eternity crept by. The pressure of his hand on my shoulder shifted, guiding me downward.

"Floor below you. Just fold your tail. That's right."

Something thudded against my scales.

The hood vanished.

I gasped, the world returning in a rush. Light glared in my eyes, white and gold by turns, while every nook and cranny for a hundred yards around suddenly made themselves known in my head.

Niall let me go. I blinked hard, the blur resolving into a

room.

An *enormous* room, filled with dehaians.

Polished white floors stretched away from me on all sides, reflecting blue-white light from chandeliers over a hundred feet above. Levels upon levels of galleries and archways formed the walls to either side of me, all of them shaped from marble and sparkling gold. Ahead, a broad stone dais stood, an ornate set of seven thrones at its top and an intricate mosaic of a blue stone mountain taking up the entire wall behind it. Dehaians with every color of scales imaginable floated in the arches and lined the floor, leaving me in an open aisle that led to the dais and the thrones.

I looked up, and my confusion melted into shock. Another dehaian sat on the largest and centermost throne.

And give or take a few decades, he looked just like an older version of Ren.

My gaze slid to the brothers, all of whom were watching the floor. From the corner of his eye, Zeke cast quick glances to me, concern and discomfort on his face.

The man rose and immediately, the others dropped into a bow.

At a loss, I dipped my head, still watching the man.

"Renekialen," he said, his voice deep and neutral as it carried through the room. "What is the meaning of this?"

"A spy, Father," Ren replied, his gaze on the floor.

Zeke's jaw muscles jumped. "She's not," he growled at Ren.

The man's eyebrow twitched up. "Zekerian?"

"She's not a spy," Zeke elaborated, his tone only barely civil.

A moment passed.

"Very well," the man acquiesced. "Then perhaps we should hear your case for why your brother is mistaken." He looked to a gray-haired dehaian with faded emerald scales who floated at the base of the dais. "In private."

The old dehaian moved immediately to the center of the aisle. Drawing himself up to the most of his relatively short height, he intoned something in a language I couldn't understand, and then paused. "This concludes the royal audience for the day," he continued in English. "His Highness, King Torvias Ociras of Yvaria, wishes you well."

The crowd swam from the room. With a controlled gesture, the gray-haired dehaian motioned us all toward a doorway near the base of the dais.

I followed the others, swimming awkwardly with my forearms still bound.

Slender-leafed plants stretched the length of the doorframe, and past them, a room waited. The space was much smaller than the one we had just left, with dark stone for the walls, another door on the opposite side, and a fireplace lit by blue-white flames in the corner. Guards took up positions around the room, while the gray-haired man waited till we all were inside and then pressed his hand to a lighter patch of stone beside the doorframe.

The long leaves of the plants stilled, taking on a solidity like wood. Turning from the door, the old dehaian floated to the corner, stoically awaiting further commands.

Ignoring him, the king looked to his sons. "Ren?"

"The girl tried to get inside the city with claims the 'Sylphaen' are chasing her, and that they gave her a drug that requires the attention of our doctors."

"*She's* not claiming that," Zeke snapped. "*I* am! Damn you, Ren, why can't you listen–"

"Zeke," his father interrupted. He turned back to Ren. "And where did you find her attempting to enter the city?"

Ren paused. "When I found her, she was with Zeke and Niall. She'd already convinced them of her story by the time I arrived."

Scowling, Zeke eyed his brother. "Oh, for the love of–"

"Zeke," the king said. "Where did you find her?"

"In Santa Lucina," Zeke replied. "Not trying to convince me of anything. She didn't even know what dehaians *were* till I told her."

Ren scoffed.

Gritting his teeth, Zeke didn't look at him. "Ask Ina. She knows all about how this started."

His dad paused. "I will check with Ina later. Now, you tell me your side and why you think a dead cult is involved."

Zeke drew a breath. "They're involved because they attacked me. And because they chained me to a wall in a cave and told me how they wanted to sacrifice her. They also said they'd had trouble finding her, and so they'd drowned a bunch of humans just trying to figure out which one was the girl they were searching for."

I looked to Zeke. I hadn't heard that the Sylphaen had grabbed him. Or that those girls...

My stomach turned. I pushed the thought away.

"They told me they planned to give her a drug," Zeke continued. "Some messed-up form of neiphiandine that they needed her to have for their 'ritual'. And when I saw her next, they had."

Ren grimaced. "There is still no proof that she was a victim of any–"

"How about the fact that the first time they tried to catch her, they put her in the hospital with so much head trauma, her human friends thought she would die? Or the fact that drug nearly killed her before she could change fully? Though I'm sure that was all just part of her master plan."

I swallowed. I knew the hospital had been bad. And I knew it'd hurt when I changed – a *lot*. I hadn't known what any of it looked like from the outside, though.

"She does strange things to the water when she touches it, Father."

My brow furrowed.

"And she's lived on land her whole life," Zeke continued. "Hundreds of miles from the ocean, and she's never *once* changed until this week." He paused. "I'm just trying to do the right thing here. Something insane is going on and I don't want more people getting hurt from it."

The king regarded him for a moment, and then his gaze

turned to me. I tried not to fidget uncomfortably.

His dark blue eyes seemed to look right through me, and I had no idea what he saw.

"What is your name, child?" he asked.

"Chloe."

"And what is it you want here, Chloe?"

My brow twitched down. "I want this drug gone so I can go home."

"Where is home?"

I paused. The answer wasn't Reidsburg. Not really. I didn't even know what the truth was anymore.

But anything else would make Zeke look bad.

"I live in Kansas," I said.

Ren looked away, clearly exasperated. "She's lying."

"I grew up there."

"No one could live that far–"

"That is enough," the king interrupted. He studied me briefly, and then glanced to his other son. "Niall? What of your opinion?"

Niall hesitated. "I didn't see any Sylphaen," he allowed, "but I saw what happened when she changed. Zeke's right. That wasn't normal. It almost killed her."

I shivered.

"This could still be–" Ren started.

His father turned to him, and he fell silent.

"Where did these Sylphaen take you?" the king asked Zeke.

"A cave, north of Anelia by a few hundred miles, and about

an hour west of the Lirian relay station."

The king nodded. He glanced to the gray-haired dehaian still waiting in the corner. "Keep her under guard."

Zeke made an angry sound.

"And put her in a room within the palace," his dad continued over the noise. "Have the royal physicians examine her."

He looked back at Zeke while the older dehaian motioned to a guard, who swam from the room.

"Thank you, Father," Zeke managed.

"You send soldiers to each border," the king told Ren, "with orders to search out any evidence that the Sylphaen have returned. Send others to locate this cave."

Ren's mouth tightened. "They are needed here, Father. The Vetorian mercenaries have—"

"Did you not hear my order, Captain of the Guard?" the king asked with a raised eyebrow.

Ren hesitated, and then grudgingly bowed his head. "I did, sire."

For a moment, the king regarded his sons, and then his blue gaze moved on to me.

"Unchain her," he ordered.

A guard came up. A key clacked inside the lock. The shackles dropped from my forearms.

I let out a breath in relief.

"Very well then, my dear," the king said. "Enjoy your stay at our home. For your sake, I hope you are not found to be a liar."

I swallowed nervously. One of the guards pressed his hand to the doorframe, turning the plants back to loosely flowing leaves, and then he and several others accompanied the king from the room. Without a word, Ren turned and left by the opposite door.

The gray-haired dehaian motioned to the open door. "This way," he intoned.

I glanced to Zeke when neither he nor Niall moved.

Closing his eyes, Zeke shook his head.

"Could've gone worse," Niall offered.

Zeke eyed him briefly and then looked to me, worry creeping into his gaze. "You okay?"

I nodded.

He released a breath, which degenerated into a scoff at the end. "Welcome to Nyciena," he said as he swam for the door.

5

ZEKE

Pushing past the fejeria in the doorway, I headed into the hall. Chloe and Niall followed me, with four of the palace guards coming behind.

I couldn't believe how my family was treating her.

Sure, I'd known Ren was uptight. Caught up in how things looked and what people thought because someday he'd take the throne. In matters of what was proper behavior for the rest of us, he was more Dad than Dad – something he seemed to take pride in.

But what he'd done to Chloe…

We didn't react like that. Shackles and gags and armed guards. We didn't do those things. Not to strangers. Not to girls who'd just shown up in our waters. Not to anyone but dehaians we *knew* were our enemies.

No matter what Ren thought of me – and I knew what he thought wasn't exactly glowing, not that I cared – we did *not* treat people like that.

I exhaled slowly, working to calm down as I followed Orvien and attempted to ignore the guards. The old chamberlain swam through the hall, never looking back while he led us toward the opposite end of the palace from the royal family's rooms.

I fought to keep from scowling.

Even at the far side of the palace, she'd have these guards on her. As much as Dad's decision to keep her under watch like a criminal angered me, I could admit it would probably make her safer too. And whether Ren liked it or not, Dad *had* ordered the guard to look for the Sylphaen, which might mean those lunatics would be too busy hiding to go after her again.

Hopefully, anyway.

"So, um…"

At Chloe's hesitant words, I glanced back. Her green eyes wide, she stared around as she trailed us through the long hallway.

I cursed myself for getting distracted. She was under enough stress with the way my family was behaving, and the palace wasn't close to anything she might have seen on land. Through the chandelier-lit water, the ceiling was a blue-gray blur over a hundred stories up. Arches on the stone walls opened onto other levels above us, and servants shot across the empty space between them. Gold and gems lined the archways and glittered in the light, while the polished stone of the walls reflected their shine. Schools of multicolored fish drifted among it all, protected from the pressure of the water's depth by the magic surrounding the city.

It had to seem bizarre.

She pulled her gaze from the palace to turn it on me. "You're a *prince*?" she asked, looking between me and Niall. "You're both…"

I hesitated. I hadn't said anything because there honestly hadn't been time. And because the question of what she was, why a bunch of psychos were after her, and how she managed to electrocute the water by touching it had all seemed far more important than the fact that, by virtue of being eight whole minutes older than Ina, I was third in line to a throne.

Though from Chloe's expression, she clearly wouldn't have agreed with me.

"Yeah," Niall supplied.

A breath left her. "Why didn't you mention that?" she asked, looking mostly to me.

I tried not to wince.

"What were you even *doing* in Santa Lucina?" she persisted. "Shouldn't you have had, like, bodyguards or a retinue or whatever? At first, I mean. Back when—"

"Your majesties," a pair of servants murmured as they moved past us in the opposite direction.

Chloe's brow climbed.

"Santa Lucina is our territory," I explained, "so it's safe. Normally, anyway."

"Your territory."

I glanced to Niall, hoping for some help.

"Part of the Yvarian State," he clarified. "Like most of the western coastline of North America. Any dehaians who aren't Dad's subjects have to receive permission to cross our borders and travel there."

She stared at him for a heartbeat. "O-okay. But... still. You're..."

I was really having trouble not wincing at how taken back she looked.

"Dad usually would insist we bring a couple guards with us, yeah," Niall admitted. "For appearance's sake, if nothing else. But Ina – that's his twin sister," he added with a nod to me, "–she likes to sneak out and party with the humans. Dad hates it when she does that, but if he sent guards, she'd just take off. Zeke's the only one she doesn't avoid till she decides to go home. And like Zeke said: usually, Santa Lucina is safe."

Chloe looked between us again, as though still attempting to get the whole situation to sink in.

"It's not that big a deal," I tried.

A half dozen dehaians bowed when we swam by.

Her gaze tracked them and then returned to me, wide-eyed.

I glanced to Orvien, willing him to swim faster to reach whatever room he'd decided she should have.

At a stately pace that would have seemed slow to a snail, the old man headed upward till he reached an archway on the thirty-fifth floor. Silently, we followed while he continued down the twisting corridor beyond the arch, stopping finally at a door partway along the stone hall.

"Your majesties," he intoned, bowing to us and then motioning to the fejeria.

Two of the guards took up positions by the door, while the other two swam inside.

Restraining a sigh, I pushed past the swaying green plants, and then noted with relief that out of the many rooms in the palace, Orvien at least hadn't put her in one of the spaces reserved for visitors we didn't want to have. Those barely qualified as closets. Instead, the place was a standard guest room, with polished stone walls about twenty-five feet high and arched windows shielded by tall stands of fejeria. Through the doorway on the far side, a sand-bed waited with blankets of woven seaweed fibers and walls of opalescent glass. Frosted crystal bowls hung from the ceiling in both rooms, the flames inside them flickering brightly.

I looked back. Chloe was eyeing it all as though she didn't know what to make of the place.

The fejeria rustled and she spun.

"It's okay," Niall assured her.

A trio of dehaians came to a stop. "Prince Nialloran. Prince Zekerian," the oldest of the three said as he and the others bowed to Niall and me in turn. He glanced to Chloe. "Hello, miss. I am Physician Kyne. These are my assistants, Tiro and Dion. I was told you needed to see us?"

Chloe looked to me.

I nodded. "This is Chloe. She's a friend of ours. Some people injected her with a modified form of neiphiandine and we need you to make sure she'll be okay."

"Modified?" Kyne asked.

"It made changing forms excruciating for her."

He studied Chloe, his gaze taking on a clinical edge. "And how long ago was she injected?"

I glanced back to her.

"Yesterday afternoon," she answered.

Kyne nodded, the slight wrinkles of his face deepening while he considered the information. "Very well. Miss, if you would join us?"

He motioned to the decorative stone table in the center of the room, and immediately, his assistants moved to place their bags where he'd directed. Chloe hesitated, her face betraying hints of her nervousness, and then she followed.

"What are you going to do?" she asked, watching as Tiro and Dion drew containers from their bags and set them on the table.

"We're just going to take some blood to start," Kyne said. He looked to the amber-scaled dehaian behind him. "Dion?"

The young man picked up one of the containers and came up beside her. "If you would hold out your arm?"

She hesitated again, eyeing the jar and Dion alike, before warily raising her arm. With careful motions, he opened the container and then used a pair of pinchers to extract a transparent creature about five inches long.

"This will only hurt a bit," Kyne told her.

She didn't take her eyes from the leech. The thing wriggled as Dion lowered it onto her skin.

It bit down. A startled gasp escaped her and I tensed at the sound, but the pain seemed to pass for her almost immediately. She drew a breath and looked back at me, clearly working to stay calm.

I gave her a smile, attempting to appear encouraging. On her arm, blood started to fill the creature's body, turning it from transparent to deep red.

"Ugh," Niall murmured.

I glanced to him in agreement.

Dion pulled the creature from her arm and transferred it back to the container. Tiro took it from him and then handed him another jar.

Niall let out a breath as the next leech bit down. "So you going to be alright keeping an eye on her?" he asked me. "I mean, when you're not just…"

I tossed him a glare, though it died quickly.

His lip twitched, but his heart didn't seem to be in it either. "Okay, well, I got stuff to take care of and, uh…" He made an uncomfortable noise as the leech was removed and another replaced it. "Right."

He swam from the room.

"You're doing well," Kyne said to Chloe. "Just one more."

She gave a tense smile, her gaze anywhere but on the thing

on her arm. "What are you going to do with these?"

"This will let us test for the differences in the neiphiandine in your system," Kyne told her. "Ordinarily, neiphiandine would not cause pain. It's simply a transformation inhibitor, designed to keep dehaians who may be suffering from a serious illness from changing into unsupportable forms while underwater."

Her brow furrowed.

"Human, dear," he elaborated while Dion removed the leech and then placed another on her skin. "Or anything close to. Between a full transformation to survive in the depths and our human forms above water, there are numerous variations – several of which would be lethal down here. Neiphiandine pushes the body into the fullest extent of change and then inhibits the ability to alter shape back again, keeping a sick dehaian from harming themselves in their delirium while this far underwater. That said, however, a single dose would never last beyond a day. Two at the most."

"And this?"

"Hopefully, it will wear off on its own as well, or we can find a treatment. We won't be certain till we run some tests."

Dion removed the creature from her arm.

"There we go," Kyne said.

He looked to me while Dion and Tiro placed the containers back in their bags. "We will let you know what we find."

"Thank you," I said.

They swam past me and left the room. By the door, the guards remained.

Chloe didn't turn around.

"Could you guys wait outside?" I said to the guards.

They hesitated and then disappeared out the door.

Silence settled over the room.

"Are you alright?" I asked her.

She didn't respond.

I grimaced, feeling like an idiot. She'd been through who-knew-what in the past week, and that was before my oldest brother decided chaining her up with a magical blindfold and shackles was the bright idea of the day.

Of course she wasn't alright.

"They're really good at what they do," I tried. "I'm sure they'll find something to help you."

She nodded.

"And I'm sorry about earlier," I continued. "Ren and... just all that."

Her head turned, though she didn't meet my eyes. "Not your fault."

"Still."

A moment passed.

"So what happens now?" she asked softly.

"You stay with us till we figure this out."

She looked back at me, and I could see the fear she was working to hide.

"They'll find a solution, Chloe. And in the meantime,

we'll–"

"You told your dad I did strange things to the water?"

I paused.

"Zeke?"

"Yeah," I allowed.

"What do I do?"

My mouth tightened. She looked so worried, though she was obviously trying not to show it. I didn't want to make things worse. "It's nothing. It's just, whenever you're–"

The fejeria rustled. I turned to see Ina poke her head into the room.

"Hey there," she called. "Hope I'm not interrupting anything? Niall said you might be busy."

Her grin made me want to scowl.

"No," I retorted. "Of course not. We were just talking."

"Oh," Ina drawled, her eyes twinkling.

I glared.

"So is this her?" she continued as she pushed past the fejeria. "I mean," Ina glanced to Chloe, "you." She laughed at herself. "Sorry. Rude, yeah? What's your name?"

"Chloe, yes," I supplied. I looked back at Chloe. "And this is my sister, Ina."

With a chuckle, Ina extended a hand. Chloe hesitated, and then shook it.

"Nice to finally meet Zeke's mystery girl." Ina's smile deepened as she looked Chloe up and down, not letting go of her hand. "You're even prettier than he said."

Chloe blinked and blushed as she glanced to me.

"Ina…" I growled.

My sister's smile took on an impish edge. "What?"

"Can we not do this?"

She gave me a mock-disappointed look. "Oh fine," she surrendered, letting Chloe's hand go. "So what were you talking about, then?"

I hesitated. "The water thing. And before you ask, no, I don't know anything more."

Ina turned back to Chloe. "So what is it?"

Chloe glanced between us. "I'm not really sure what you mean," she said cautiously.

"Things feel different around you," I explained. "Like… like there's a charge to the water."

Her brow rose.

"It's not so much right now," I tried.

"I can't even tell it's there anymore," Ina added.

I gave her a frustrated glance before continuing. "I noticed it the first time I saw you, though. You were on the beach with that human guy. The one in the water yesterday. Your feet touched the waves and…" I shrugged. "I could feel it."

"Me too," Ina said. "And I was a mile or so away."

Chloe stared at us.

"I'm guessing you didn't know, though," I finished.

Her expression didn't change.

"What did Dad think about all this?" Ina asked into the silence.

"He's the one who put the guards on her."

"Huh. Well, um… what about Granddad? Maybe he'll know something."

I paused. "Jirral's here? You've talked to him?"

She had the grace to look embarrassed. "Not yet. But he sends me letters occasionally. And he's back in the area now. Has been since last week." She shrugged. "I was going to tell you. I just…"

I looked away. I could understand why she hadn't said anything. Even if I hadn't been in Santa Lucina, it wasn't simply a question of seeing him.

It was a question of whether or not any of us would want to.

I let out a breath, feeling the pressure of Chloe's confusion as she looked between us. Everything else aside – and 'everything else' contained a lot – Jirral was one of the most connected people I knew. He travelled the entire ocean and counted as friends more people than I'd met in my entire life. If anyone had heard of somebody like Chloe, it'd be him.

Even if I'd rather have discussed this with the Sylphaen than him.

"Where is he?" I asked.

"A house near the city wall."

"That close?"

"I think he wants to try to make peace with Dad again."

I watched her for a moment. She shrugged.

Taking a breath, I shook my head and then glanced to

Chloe. "Care to meet more of my family?"

She looked skeptical. I couldn't blame her.

Not knowing what else to say, I headed for the door. The guards would probably want to come – something that would upset Jirral to no end. But there was no way to get them to stay here, so we'd just have to deal with it.

Which was sure to be fun.

Grimacing, I swam out of the room.

❧ 6 ❧

CHLOE

With guards surrounding us, I trailed Zeke and Ina down the hall. The girl looked like her brothers – all dark hair, sapphire eyes, and features so sharp they could probably cut something. Unlike what wrapped my stomach and chest, the opalescent gunmetal of her scales ended at her hips, where they became skin again. A faux-bikini top of scales covered her chest, the back of which gave up the illusion and twisted off across the silver sheen of her skin like an exotic tribal tattoo. An amused smile hovered around her lips, the expression reminiscent of Niall, as if the world was a joke out of which she was determined to get the most enjoyment she could.

And she was royalty. Her brothers were royalty.

I'd been talking with, and swimming with, and generally following *royalty*.

No matter how I tried, I couldn't quite wrap my head around it, any more than I could understand what Zeke had said about me and the water. How could I be doing something and not realize it? Sending a charge through the ocean strong enough that Ina had felt it over a mile away?

It didn't make sense.

I turned with them at the archway, swimming down past level upon level of the palace. The whole building was enormous, to the point that the White House and Buckingham Palace could probably have taken corners and still barely made a dent in all the room to spare. How it went unnoticed at the bottom of the ocean, I didn't know, except I was starting to suspect that like the lights and the veils and the fact I had a long tail where my legs should be, there was probably some kind of magic involved.

Though again, that should have been impossible.

Like everything else.

I shook my head, trying to stop my thoughts from spinning. We were heading for a larger door at the end of the hall, and the plants blocking this one were easily twice the height of all the others I'd seen. Without much more than a nod to the guards hovering on either side, Zeke and Ina pushed by the green stands of leaves. Two of the guards with us went ahead of me, with the others waiting to follow behind.

Attempting to keep from looking nervous, I swam after Zeke and his sister. Beyond the door, sand and rock stretched out for a hundred yards, decorated with torches and carved stones and ending at a wall with a glittering veil rising from its top. I looked back as we left, seeing the enormity of the place for the first time.

It was a mountain.

Or most of a mountain. In the pale blue twilight created by the torches and the reflection from the veil, I could see the slope rising above the ocean floor, until distance and the water obscured it. Windows peppered the rocky sides, with swaying plants in all of them, while dehaians darted from opening to opening, weaving across the mountainside as though it was just another way of getting around the palace.

"He's about a block shy of the outside wall," Ina said.

I turned back as Zeke nodded and glanced to one of the guards. The man went ahead of us, and then did something to the veil.

The bubbles parted like a curtain. Zeke and Ina swam up, cresting the top of the wall and continuing on. I followed them.

And then I had to work not to stare.

Natural rock arches and spires of skyscraper proportions spread out before me, their walls twisted and curved as though shaped by centuries of gently eroding water. Windows and doors speckled their sides, with plants blocking the entrances. Tall streetlights lined the pathways between the houses and shops, and their blue-white flames reflected from the rainbow colors of ore buried within the stone walls. A veil as large as the sky arched over the entire city, the distant bubbles twinkling like stars as they caught the torchlight.

"Nice, huh?" Ina said.

I blinked and looked over to find her and Zeke watching

me.

"How…" I cleared my throat. "How does all this stay hidden?"

Zeke glanced to his sister and then shrugged. "Magic."

I swallowed. Right.

"This way," Ina said. She swam down a twisting path between two stone arches bigger than any of the buildings in my hometown.

Zeke paused, still watching me. "You okay?"

Drawing a breath, I nodded. We followed Ina.

Conversations and music carried from within the buildings we passed, if the enormous structures could be called that. Behind curtains of tall green leaves, I could hear children calling to their parents and people laughing. Every so often, a dehaian would slip out from between the leaves, only to stop and bow the moment they caught sight of Ina and Zeke. Their gazes trailed us when we swam on, the curiosity at the guards and my presence blatant on their faces.

Minutes later, the lower reaches of the veil came into view. I couldn't see anything past it; the bubbles were more numerous here and their glitter obscured the ocean beyond. But through gaps between the buildings around us, I spotted the low wall of boulders that formed its base, the ring of which continued onward, surrounding the entire city.

At a shorter block of stone a few streets away from the barrier, Ina slowed. Blue torchlight flickered in the gaps between the leaves on the windows, though unlike elsewhere in the city, this place was silent.

Ina glanced to Zeke, and then approached the nearest opening in the wall.

"Hello?" she called.

No one answered her.

She cast a quick look around. "Granddad?" she tried.

"Ina?" came a deep, hoarse voice.

A hand pulled the leaves back to reveal a weathered face with dark blue eyes. Gray hair long enough to brush his cheekbones hung from the man's head in loose strands, and old scars puckered the skin of his chest and arms.

At the sight of Zeke, the man paused, a cautious look replacing the nascent friendliness in his expression. "Zeke."

"Jirral."

I glanced over. Zeke's voice was cold, and his face matched the sound.

The old man's gaze took in me and the guards before returning to his grandson. "What are you doing here?"

"We need to talk to you," Ina told him.

"Talk to me," he repeated, still watching Zeke. "And you brought guards."

The muscles jumped in Zeke's jaw. "Not our choice."

I could see the disbelief in the man's eyes.

"Granddad, please," Ina said. "They're here because of her, not you. And she's why we need to talk. Can we come in?"

He paused, his gaze twitching to me. "They stay outside." He jerked his chin at the guards.

Ina glanced over. The nearest one hesitated, and then bowed his head.

The old man backed from the opening, allowing us to enter.

A bleak room greeted us, with hardly more than empty walls and a fireplace to its name. The ceiling was lower than I'd seen in most dehaian spaces so far, which meant it was almost normal height for a human. A bag was placed in the corner and a stone chest sat nearby, but beyond those two small features, the place was utterly bare.

Ina looked around, a hint of sadness darkening the normal humor in her eyes. "How've you been?" she asked quietly.

Jirral paused as the leaves closed up behind us. Pity softened his hard expression. "Fine, poppet. What's this about?"

Ina looked to Zeke. He didn't take his gaze from the nearly empty room. "We've got kind of an odd question," she sighed. "Have you ever met anyone who, you know, does strange things to the water? Makes it feel different around them?"

The old man glanced to me with the same piercing gaze that Zeke's father possessed.

I tried not to look too nervous.

"How so?" he asked.

"Like there's electricity in the water," Ina said. "Like a charge is running through the whole ocean."

"Is this why there were guards on her?"

"Sort of," Ina allowed.

Jirral waited. She grimaced.

"Care to help me out here?" she asked Zeke.

Pulling his attention from the room, Zeke glanced to her, his face tense. "Dad put guards on her because Ren thinks she's a spy," he supplied shortly. "He didn't believe me when I said she was being chased by a group of Sylphaen and needed our help."

His grandfather's eyebrow rose, and Zeke's mouth tightened. "We don't know if it's related to them," he continued, "and it's practically undetectable now, but every time Chloe's gotten in the water," he nodded toward me, "there's been this strange feeling like Ina described. We need to know if you've ever heard of someone who could do that."

The old man paused. "Not that I recall."

"Alright then." Zeke turned for the door.

"Zeke," Ina protested.

"So that's it?" his grandfather asked. "You just leave?"

"What else is there?" Zeke retorted.

"Conversation? A chance to talk? I haven't seen you in years."

"And? You've known where to find us. You've been sending messages to Ina, for pity's sake. It obviously wasn't that complicated."

"Ina made it clear she wanted to talk to me."

"Yeah, well, Ina's always been more forgiving than I am."

His sister made an angry noise. Zeke ignored it, heading for the door.

"Zeke, stop," the old man snapped. "Stop this. For ten years, you've been acting as if I wanted this to happen, just like your father and your brothers and everyone else short of Ina here. Give it a rest. I did everything I could for Miri. *Everything.* You think I wanted things to turn out the way they did?"

"You let them take her!"

I blinked at the rage in Zeke's voice.

Jirral was silent for a heartbeat. "If I hadn't, they would've killed her on the spot and taken you or Ina in her place. I–"

"You don't know that!"

"I do. I know how they operate."

Disgust twitched across Zeke's face. "No kidding."

His grandfather's face darkened. "I will not defend myself to you, Zeke. Not about that. Not when your father–"

Zeke swam for the door.

An infuriated noise left Jirral. "I know about the Sylphaen," he called.

I looked back toward him as Zeke paused.

"There are rumors, out in the Prijoran Zone. Rumors that they're back."

Zeke didn't turn around. "And do you know anything more than that?"

The old man took a breath. "They're careful. Given that they were nearly exterminated a century ago, they've taken to staying well out of sight, so I can only go on the whispers I've heard. But there are stories they're trying to find allies among the outcasts and the mercenaries. That they're trying to start over again."

"Start what?" Zeke asked.

"Their 'cleansing'. Their new world. The Sylphaen were mostly destroyed by the time I was born, but I know what my father said they were like in his day." He sighed. "A cult without any law or morality but their own. Their nonsense was tangled up in old legends, stories of ancient disasters and landwalkers, and some doomsday tale regarding both."

I swallowed. Jirral's gaze flicked to me, catching the slight motion.

"They were merciless, though," he continued with barely a pause. "The shadow court of every territory and province from here to Lycera, 'disappearing' any man, woman, or child they felt violated their code. They're obsessed with dehaian supremacy, believing that anyone who 'consorts' with humans or anything of the land taints our supposed purity, and back then, they had the numbers and the power to enforce that idea."

He glanced to me again. "But as to why they've fixated on your friend here…" He watched me with those blue eyes that seemed to just see right through everything. "What was it they wanted from you?"

I looked to Zeke, discomforted. I didn't know this man. True, he was related to Zeke and Ina, but then so was Ren. Given that, and the tension between him and his grandson, I wasn't exactly certain I could trust him.

And that was assuming I even knew what to say. The Sylphaen had called me an abomination. They'd called me the daughter of a landwalker whore. They'd said a lot of things, and if Jirral was right, that probably had to do with their obsession with dehaian purity or whatever.

But they'd also injected me with drugs to make me change and talked about a ceremony. They'd dragged a bunch of human girls under the water and killed them, simply to figure out which one was me.

And before he'd died, one of them had said something about a Beast waiting...

I shivered. I didn't want to say that. I didn't even want to *remember* it. And telling a man I didn't know about what'd happened, a man that Zeke didn't really seem comfortable around...

"They're crazy," I replied with a tense shrug.

Jirral's mouth tightened. "And this thing my grandchildren say you do?"

I tried for another shrug. "I don't—"

"That it?" Zeke cut in.

The old man turned to him. "I want to help here, Zeke. If they're after her, then you need to make Torvias understand: the Sylphaen won't stop. They were single-minded as hell in their heyday, and I doubt they've changed. If they learn she's here, you're all in danger."

"Dad has the royal guard out looking—"

"What were their stories?" I interrupted.

They both looked to me, and while Zeke seemed cautious, Jirral's eyes just narrowed.

"The doomsday stories," I pressed.

"Old myths," the man said. "Stories of beings called land-walkers, people that looked human but were actually the opposite to us in every way. In these stories, landwalkers and dehaians had once been the same. We travelled deep inland without getting sick, and they swam in the ocean just as we do. But some ancient event split us apart, creating these distinct sides." He paused. "The Sylphaen believe in all that, except to them, the landwalkers are impure – worse even than humans – and thieves who stole our ability to stay above land. They want to take that back from the landwalkers. They think that if they don't, the landwalkers will try to take our abilities instead, and somehow, the result will recreate the disaster and bring our world to an end."

Zeke made an annoyed sound. "So in short, their beliefs are psychotic and so are they. Which we already knew. Thanks for the information."

"Insane or not, the Sylphaen believe it, and that's more than enough to make them dangerous."

Grimacing, Zeke looked away.

I shivered.

"Do you know anything about this?" Jirral asked me.

Awkwardly, I glanced to Zeke. "N-no, not really. I was just curious."

I could read the doubt in the man's eyes.

"We should go," Zeke said.

"You need to tell Torvias," Jirral insisted. "Make him post extra guards around the palace."

Zeke glanced to Ina. "Maybe."

He turned, pushing aside the leaves blocking the door.

"It was good to see you again," his grandfather said.

Zeke hesitated, and then swam from the room.

"It was good to see you too," Ina replied quietly.

I followed her as she pushed the plants aside and left.

"Whatever it is," the old man called.

In the doorway, I looked back.

"I can tell you know," he continued. "At least something of what they're after, you know. And if you let it hurt my grandchildren…"

A chill ran through me at the threat in his eyes.

"I don't," I managed.

And I fled out the door.

Zeke was a hundred yards ahead of us by the time I made it outside, though the guards hadn't moved. They fell in around me the moment I swam past the doorway and boxed me in on four sides.

Still shivering from the look in the old man's eyes, I tried to ignore them. Zeke had to be right; the Sylphaen couldn't get here. With the guards I'd seen everywhere, they'd have to bring an army just to get past the front door. And that was assuming Ren didn't find something to change his mind out there, and maybe convince him I wasn't a spy after all.

There were plenty of reasons not to worry, no matter what Jirral said.

Clinging to the thought, I continued on. Ina kept pace with me, still glancing back to her grandfather's door with unhappiness lingering in her eyes.

The veil on the palace wall parted when we reached it, letting us back into the courtyard. At the door, Zeke paused, waiting for us to catch up.

"I'm going to ask Dad to put more guards around the palace," he said, grimacing. "Ina, could you…"

"Hang out?" she offered, humor coming back into her tone.

"I'll be fine," I told them both, hating the feeling that I was some child they had to keep an eye on. "The guards can–"

"Oh, please," Ina replied, her amusement strengthening. "It'll be fun."

She hooked her arm through mine and started toward the palace door, pulling me with her. As we swam by Zeke, she looked past me to meet his eyes, and I could see a hint of something less lighthearted tinge her gaze.

And then we were inside and the expression was gone.

"So," Ina said. Dehaians paused around us, bowing and watching as we passed by. She ignored them. "Where are you from? No one's told me anything beyond, you know, the weird water thing."

I hesitated. "Kansas."

Her brow furrowed.

"It's one of the middle states," I supplied.

The confusion became skepticism. "Seriously?"

I nodded, and then looked back toward the door. Zeke was nowhere to be seen.

"He'll be fine," Ina assured me. "So how'd you deal with being so far from the ocean?"

I shrugged.

"Did you, like, make saltwater in a bathtub or something so you could change shape or…"

I shook my head. "I never needed to. I just found out about dehaians last week."

She paused. "Ah."

"What?"

"Oh, nothing."

I glanced to her. She rolled her eyes.

"Really," she acquiesced. "It's just… well, that explains it a bit."

My brow furrowed incredulously. Of all the responses I'd gotten so far – including being flat-out called a liar – I hadn't expected anyone to say that. "Explains what a bit?"

Her mouth tightened as we headed up toward the level where they'd given me a room to use. "You're just not very… dehaian."

I tensed. "What do you mean?"

She didn't answer, swimming on till we reached the room. At the door, she paused, glancing to the guards. "Guys, hang out here, eh?"

Without waiting to see if they agreed, she tugged me after her into the room. On the other side of the plants, she released me and slapped a hand to a small discoloration on the stone doorframe. The leaves stilled, taking on the texture and solidity of wood.

"Let me guess," she pronounced. "My suddenly and *inexplicably* conservative brother knows you've somehow managed to be new to all this, but in spite of that, he didn't tell you anything about us. About what we are or what we can do."

I gave a small shrug. The room had seemed big before, but it felt the size of a matchbox with her in it now.

The girl was like a force of nature when she wasn't distracted by her family.

Ina sighed, rolling her eyes again as she started to swim back and forth, almost like pacing. "It's fine. It's obvious. I mean... maybe you're just modest as hell or reserved or something but..."

I looked at her in confusion.

She gestured to me. "You're so quiet. And then there's the scale thing. I mean, you know we can do what we want with that, right? In the water, out of the water..."

At my silence, she shook her head. "Okay, listen. One, you've got to loosen up. Dehaians... we know how to party. It's kind of our thing. Topside and inland? Yeah, they can be all uptight. But here?" She grinned. "Life's too short for that. We live longer than humans, but it *still* is.

"And two," she continued, "we can control these things. The scales. Out of the water, they can become like human swimsuits. Help you blend in till you can find some clothes since, you know, folks tend to frown on the whole public nudity thing, typically speaking. You can even change your feet to handle the terrain till you find shoes, because let's face it, rocks, hot sand, and whatever just aren't that fun. And in the water…"

She paused, and the skin of her torso changed, the vaguely tribal markings from the back of her faux-bikini suddenly growing and twisting across her stomach and arms like vines.

"You can get creative," she said as the shapes faded back into skin. "And trust me, the boys find it all *kinds* of sexy."

I could feel a blush creep across my face.

Her grin widened. "Come on, give it a shot. I mean, honestly. You look like you're in some kind of scale apron."

I hesitated, irritation taking the place of my embarrassment. I'd known I was dehaian for less than a week, and already I was getting criticized over their version of how I dressed?

Zeke's sister or not, it was suddenly very hard not to start disliking her.

Ina's eyebrow rose as she waited.

I drew a breath and attempted to concentrate on making the cream scales on my stomach change.

Nothing happened.

Ina's brow furrowed. "Are you trying?"

"Yes," I said, fighting to keep from snapping.

"Huh," she commented.

"The Sylphaen gave me something. Neiphiandine."

Her confusion faltered. "Oh. Uh, I'm sorry. I didn't…"

"It's fine," I said tightly.

"Well, after that clears up then. You just think of what you want, and it'll happen."

I nodded for lack of any other response to give. Hopefully the neiphiandine would wear off. Sometime soon anyway.

"But still," she said, regrouping. "You have *no* idea how good things are down here. Drugs or not, you can still enjoy it. And if you ever *do* get bored, you can always head topside once that neiphiandine goes away and just hang out there for a while. Come back when *that* gets boring, but meet all kinds of fun people in the meantime." She grinned again. "Just make sure you don't get *too* carried away. You wouldn't want to slip up and make someone fall for you."

My brow furrowed.

"Eh, magic," she explained with a wave of her hand, as though she didn't really want to dwell on it. "Aveluria's what we call it. Makes things all heightened and exciting with other dehaians, but humans react to it like a drug. You get too caught up with one of them, you might lose control of it. Get them to fall for you, hard. And then that poor soul's going to pine away, not wanting food, water, anything till they just die of longing for you. Which totally sucks, and also will get you in heaps of trouble down here, since it's super illegal and basically murder."

I stared at her.

"Don't worry," she assured me. "You mostly have to *want* magic to happen for it to work. And if you're careful and you don't let yourself get too wrapped up with them, you'll be fine – and so will they."

I managed a nod.

Her grin returned. "Okay, well," she continued, setting the topic aside. "I don't know what you had planned, but you really should let me introduce you to some people. Show you how dehaians have fun, eh?"

"What about the guards?"

She gave the door a dismissive look. "Oh, they can come. Probably do them some good, not just floating in the hall all day."

I hesitated. Given at least half the dehaians I'd met so far, I wasn't really sure I *wanted* to get to know any more of them.

But I didn't have a good excuse to stay.

"Alright," I allowed.

The guards fell in around us as I followed her from the room, and they didn't once question Ina for bringing me with her. At the massive central corridor between the many levels of the palace, she turned downward, weaving a path through the bowing servants and guards toward a wide archway on the first floor.

I slowed in shock when we reached it. Easily five stories

high, the cavernous chamber beyond was lined with white marble and gold accents. Dehaians were everywhere, resting in groups on cushions on the ground or secluded in booths perched high on the walls. Lights shone far overhead, illuminating the people scattered below, while on the opposite end of the room, a woman hovered above a platform halfway up the wall as if she was on a stage.

She was singing. I could hear it, despite the buzz of myriad conversations between us, and somehow, her voice wove them all into her song. Dropping below the murmurs and then rising above them again, she seemed to anticipate every change around her and turn it into something beautiful.

I looked to Ina. She grinned. "Nice, huh? Siren song. Part of that aveluria thing I was telling you about – though unless you've touched someone with magic first, the vocal stuff is mostly just for show. Pretty and attractive, but won't really do much. Touch is where it's really powerful."

Ina started into the room, only to pull up short as the crowd parted ahead of us.

"What?" I asked warily.

"Oh, nothing," she replied as several nearby dehaians rose from their cushions and bowed to her. "Some people had to leave court early today, I guess."

She drew a breath, pushing any trace of hesitation from her face, and grinned at me again. "It's fine. But watch out for the Deiliora twins. Especially Siracha."

Without explaining what she meant, she continued across

the room, ignoring the bows and 'your majesties' that followed her. Surrounded by guards, I trailed after her, till we reached four dehaians reclining on multicolored cushions of woven seaweed.

"Princess!" a bronze-scaled young man exclaimed when she came close. "We were beginning to think you'd forgotten us today."

Ina laughed as he embraced her. "Never," she promised.

"You've been gone too long, your highness," a young man with blue scales and copper hair said, rising as well and kissing her cheek.

"Tiago, you're such a charmer," she replied.

"Who's your friend?" the gorgeous girl next to them asked, brushing a floating strand of her blonde hair away from her shoulder. Another girl sat to her right, obviously her twin.

I tried not to tense at the way both girls looked me over like they were running some sort of evaluation.

"Oh, come on, Siracha," her sister said. "Haven't you heard? This is the girl Prince Zekerian brought back from California."

Siracha's brow rose. "The spy?"

I glanced to Ina, hoping for help. "I'm not a spy."

The blonde girl chuckled like I'd said something funny.

"Welcome," the bronze-scaled young man said, his gaze running over me too, though his expression was anything but similar to the girls'. "My name is Count Velior."

I wanted to turn around and leave.

"This is Chloe," Ina supplied. "*Not* a spy. And new here. She, um, she's from a tiny little place really far from Nyciena, and she's hardly ever met another dehaian."

Siracha's red lips curved. "Country girl. How cute."

"Be nice, Siracha," her twin admonished. She looked to me. "You'll have to excuse my sister. She really hoped *she'd* be the next girl the prince took an interest in, if you know what I mean."

"Neria!" her sister protested.

The girl just laughed.

I looked between them all, but Ina just shook her head, Tiago was focused on Ina, and Velior hadn't stopped watching me.

The door felt really far away.

"Have a seat," Ina said as she sank down. Her long gun-metal tail flicked out over a few of the cushions, and her fin moved idly in the infinitesimal current. Tiago's hand strayed over, brushing her scales, and she smiled.

Reluctantly, I joined her, keeping as far from the others as I could.

"So princess," Tiago asked, still running his fingertips along her tail. "How was Santa Lucina? We heard that the prince had an adventure, but we've scarcely seen you since you came back."

Ina smiled. "It was interesting," she allowed. "Though not as interesting as my brother's time there, obviously."

"Obviously," Velior commented.

Ina ignored him. "I did come across a nice shop, however. Brand new—"

"Princess," Neria murmured. Her gaze twitched over, and Ina followed it.

From the other side of the room, a young man with silver scales and nearly white hair watched us.

Ina sighed. "Give me a minute."

"You're too nice to him," Neria told her.

Ina tossed her a look like she agreed, but she still swam across the room. One of the guards followed her while, seeming as though he'd like to do the same, Tiago watched her go.

"That boy will get his family in such trouble if he doesn't give up following the princess around," Neria said. "Especially after upsetting her with that argument a few weeks back."

"Egan's from Teariad," Siracha replied. "What do you expect? They're all pea-brained romantics."

Her sister grinned.

"So Chloe," Velior said, still eyeing me. "We're having a party later. You should come."

"Please, Velior," Siracha cut in. "She's the prince's girl, remember? Do give him *one* day to tire of his little country tryst."

"Siracha!" Neria chastised.

"She could still come," Velior replied with a smile. "After all, she has all night to join him in his bed."

I blinked, heat racing up to color my cheeks. "Um, Zeke

and I aren't, uh…"

Siracha laughed, a scornful and knowing expression on her face.

I looked away, uncertain whether to be offended or embarrassed. Or both. I'd met these people five seconds ago, and already they'd concluded I was sleeping with the prince of their kingdom.

What the hell?

"E-excuse me," I said, rising from the cushions.

"What did we say?" Siracha called.

Ignoring her, I headed for the door, and the guards moved immediately to stay near me.

Ina swam up as I reached the far side of the room. "What happened? You alright?"

I stared at her, incredulous. "Fine, except they all seem to think I'm sleeping with your brother."

Ina paused. "Oh, they were just joking around."

I could read the fact she'd thought it too on her face. I turned away.

"Hey," Ina said, catching my arm.

I looked back at her.

Her face twisted with frustration. "I'm sorry, alright? Zeke's bringing you back with him is the latest bit of gossip, and everyone just assumed…" She shrugged expressively.

I headed out the door.

She swam after me. "Chloe," she called.

A guard cut me off, forcing me to stop.

Ina pulled up alongside me and waved him off.

"Come here," she told me, gesturing to an alcove in the wall.

Without many other options, I followed her. The guards automatically formed a perimeter around us, keeping the servants and courtiers away.

"Look," Ina sighed. "No one meant anything by it." She paused. "Well, besides Siracha. The girl's a snake, though of course she doesn't let my brothers see that. And Velior just wants whatever he thinks the princes have. It's not personal. But Zeke... he likes you, okay? I can tell. Two seconds around him and I can tell, even if for *some* reason he apparently hasn't admitted it to you or himself."

My brow furrowed. He'd never shown the least sign of that.

Ina didn't pause. "And I'm guessing a lot of the girls who are used to getting his attention will notice it soon too, if they haven't already. So they're going to assume things. It's kind of our nature. Human nature too, for that matter."

I struggled to keep from grimacing and mostly failed.

"Don't let it bother you," Ina finished.

I managed a nod, though the grimace didn't fade.

A small noise of frustration escaped her, and I followed her gaze to the silver-scaled young man. He was swimming toward us again.

"Guys?" Ina said to the guards.

One of them separated from the group and moved to

intercept him.

"Let's go to my apartment," Ina continued to me. "Court's boring today."

Without waiting for a response, she swam up through the main corridor. The guards around me, I followed.

Dehaians bowed as always when she passed, but now I felt their gazes trailing us more than ever. How many knew the palace gossip?

A trio of snobbish-looking courtiers swam by, bowing to the princess and then studying me as we continued on.

I tried not to sigh. Probably all of them.

Not that it mattered, honestly. Ren's belief I was a spy was a *much* more critical problem than the opinions of a bunch of dehaian busybodies.

It was just annoying.

Really annoying. Now that I watched for it, I could see courtiers whispering behind their hands as we passed, while their gazes tracked me with knowing expressions. What was it with these people? How was it that everyone just *assumed*, because I traveled here with Zeke, we were '*obviously*' having sex?

Though that sort of made me wonder about him in general.

I shook the thought off. His life was none of my business. For that matter, whether or not he liked me was irrelevant too. I didn't think about Zeke that way. And not because he wasn't attractive – God *knew* Zeke was attractive – but because he was part of this world, a world I'd never planned on joining and that I fully intended to leave as soon as possible. And because there was Noah to consider, even if I wasn't really confident about in what terms. He'd kissed me, yes. I liked him a lot. But I wasn't sure I could claim we were dating. I mean, I'd *like* to. I *wanted* to. In my book, a kiss like that *pretty* much put you in the category of dating a guy. But I also wasn't certain what Noah thought and I didn't want to get ahead of myself. After all, that kiss could have meant less to him than it had to me. He could have just been caught up in the moment or whatever. But regardless, I wasn't going to just *forget* him and go checking out some other guy now that I was down here. It'd only been a *day*, for pity's sake. That was ridiculous.

And Zeke had never given a single sign he thought of me as anything other than some girl he was helping. At best, he was my friend and nothing more.

Not that it even mattered anyway.

Feeling like my mind was steadily becoming a pretzel, I kept myself from looking at any more courtiers as I followed Ina back to her room.

～ 7 ～

ZEKE

It took me a moment after Chloe and Ina disappeared through the door to want to move.

And a few moments beyond that to gather my thoughts enough to swim up toward the royal suite.

I wished I could claim seeing Jirral had been a waste of time. It would've been easier. And while, yes, most of it *had* been useless, that part about the Sylphaen...

Shaking my head, I continued upward along the face of the mountain toward the entrances to the top floors. The cult couldn't reach us here. All the psychotic beliefs and purifying crusades in the world wouldn't get them past the soldiers surrounding Nyciena.

Though adding a few more guards couldn't hurt.

Not that I was about to tell Jirral that.

Servants bowed and leaves of fejeria swayed as I passed. The veil around the palace deadened any sense of the surrounding water and cast a silvery sheen on the mountainside.

Up above, I spotted Dad's guards near the opening to his floors – a good sign that he was there and not off holding another audience with whichever nobles had come to town today.

"Prince Zekerian!"

I slowed and glanced back at the shout from below.

Kyne hovered by one of the windows. When he saw me stop, he pushed away from the opening and swam after me.

"We have preliminary results of the tests, highness," he said. "Do you have a moment?"

I nodded. "What'd you find out?"

"The mixture is strange. Mostly neiphiandine, but with supplementary agents that appear designed to make it stronger, longer-lasting, and even less likely to be affected or overcome by stresses to the system."

I grimaced. Those Sylphaen bastards wanted to *sacrifice* her. I'd call that a stress to her system. Why they needed to make sure she stayed in dehaian form while that happened, though...

"How long-lasting?" I asked, pushing the thought aside.

"It's difficult to say. It would depend upon the young lady's metabolism, her body chemistry, factors of that sort. But that brings up something else strange. In addition to this, there are other components to the drug. We haven't yet determined their purpose, but in our tests, they seem to act as suppressants of some kind. It may be that they were intended to keep her body from flushing out the drug, or there may have been another intent behind their inclusion. We will need to run additional tests to be–"

"Yeah," I interrupted. "Just… whatever you need to do to help her."

Kyne bowed. "Thank you, highness."

I nodded. Taking the motion as a dismissal, he turned and disappeared behind the fejeria of another window.

Drawing a deep breath, I kept going toward the soldiers above me. We needed more guards. More *anything* to keep those bastards from having a chance at whatever it was they wanted.

The soldiers moved aside when I reached them and the dark walls of the upper floor hallway closed around me as I continued onward. Compared to the lower levels, or even the nearby floors that held our own apartments, the décor up here seemed more subdued. The marble and gold accenting were gone, replaced by deep brown stone. The appearance was deceptive, however. Gold inlay traced wire-thin lines through the rock, picking out designs of all the territories of Yvaria, though the patterns only became clear when you passed and the light caught them a certain way. Tiny gemstones did the same, speckling every square inch of the corridor in a display that, as you swam along it, began to look like a child's fantasy vision of a jewel mine. Bowls of translucent opal hung from the ceiling, holding flames that made the walls sparkle, and starbursts of larger gems surrounded them.

Dad knew what it was to impress, and leave no one who visited with any doubt of just *how* much wealth and territory he controlled.

Two more guards hovered outside the door of Dad's personal audience chamber – the place in which all the nobles tirelessly bargained and clamored to be received, though only the elite few ever were.

"Is he available?" I asked them.

"Dinner has just arrived," one replied. "Allow me to see if he wishes company."

"Thanks."

The man turned and slipped through the fejeria leaves.

A moment passed.

"–and I'm telling you two-person teams are enough. We don't need to waste resources chasing my brother's delusions, understand?"

I glanced over. At the far end of the corridor, near the opening to the rest of the castle, Ren swam out into the hall from one of Dad's study rooms. A soldier followed, bearing the same tense and obedient look on his face that all the guards adopted when my brother was around.

"Yes, sir," the man answered with a nod.

Ren turned and headed back inside.

I scowled, furious at his words despite my relief he hadn't noticed me. I didn't need another argument right now. Not when it was obvious what he'd say to the idea of even more guards against the Sylphaen.

The fejeria rustled as the guard returned.

"He will see you, highness," the man said.

I nodded and swam by him.

On a cushioned seat behind a broad table, Dad was scanning over a collection of reports, his brow wrinkled with displeasure. A silver tray of food rested nearby, most of it already gone, and additional stacks of paper-thin, bleached seaweed lay on the table, the writing on them indecipherable from where I stood.

"Thank you for seeing me, Father," I said, bowing uncomfortably.

He didn't look away from the reports in his hand. "I have officials from Ryaira coming in ten minutes to discuss their ongoing border dispute with Teariad. What did you need to ask me about?"

"The Sylphaen. I—"

"Your brother is sending people out within the hour, Zeke. We've already settled this."

"I know, but I'd like to request additional guards around the palace."

He glanced up at me. "Why?"

I hesitated. I couldn't bring up Jirral. Dad would dismiss any idea that came from him out of hand.

Not that I'd blame him. Ordinarily, anyway.

"As a precaution," I said. "If the Sylphaen are back, there's no guarantee they haven't gotten inside the borders already. I want to make certain the capital is protected."

Dad paused. "We will be safe here, Zeke. I know you and he have difficulties, but Ren is more attentive to our intelligence network than you give him credit for. Before you came home, he'd already put the palace guard on alert about potential Vetorian spies and taken measures to secure any leaks in the border. Those measures will serve against anyone, Sylphaen or not."

"Father, I—"

"Zeke, it will be sufficient." He sighed. "You should have listened to your brother and come home, especially in light of how you were attacked. I appreciate that you wish to help this girl, but no one is worth the safety of a member of the royal family. You and Niall both, I would have expected you to understand that."

I worked hard to keep from scowling, and not just because of the way the words stung. What should I have done? I'd been the only one who knew what Chloe looked like, who'd recognize her friends, or who'd seen the bastards after her. The guards could have hunted forever to find her, only to have the Sylphaen get away with Chloe ¬in the meantime.

Dad set the reports aside. "Son, we will find the ones responsible, and regardless, they will not endanger us here. And whether they are trying to resurrect that dead cult or not, rest assured I will see them punished for what they did to you."

I couldn't stop the grimace this time. I knew what Dad's version of 'punished' looked like. I'd rather it never happened again. And in the meantime, I didn't want my request being dismissed as some trauma over being grabbed by the Sylphaen.

"It's not about that. I'm fine. But these guys are—"

"Enough." He shook his head, his brow furrowing as though something bothered him. "Increasing the guard further will only serve to frighten the populace and create an impression that we doubt Yvaria's strength. I will not–"

His brow furrowed again. A cough escaped him and he tapped a fist to his chest, as though trying to dislodge something in his throat.

"Are you alright?" I asked.

Grimacing, he nodded. "Fine, I just–"

The cough came again, harder. His hand grasped the edge of the table as he doubled over.

I hesitated, nearly two decades worth of training that forbid me from touching the king holding me paralyzed. "Hey," I called to the guards outside, not taking my eyes from him. I made myself swim closer. "Are you sure you–"

He choked, tumbling from the seat.

I rushed to him, weaving around the table fast. Grabbing his arms, I tried to help him up from the floor. His hands clamped down, digging hard into my forearms as he looked up at me.

His skin was splotchy. Blue and purple in turns from veins breaking inside. Blood vessels had burst in his eyes, staining them red, and his chest spasmed as he fought to breathe. His mouth was moving, forming words I couldn't hear, and fear subsumed every other expression on his face.

"Help!" I yelled.

I looked to the door as the guards rushed in.

"Get a physician!"

Their eyes went wide and one of them spun fast, racing from the room.

Dad convulsed, his hands clenching on my arms, and I turned back to see his bloodied eyes go wide. He gasped, pain tightening his face as his gaze went past me to the ceiling with a look of terror.

Which faded. Melted away, becoming a sort of hideous confusion. He trembled, his brow drawing down, while something almost like sorrow drifted through his eyes.

And then it evaporated like smoke, leaving nothing.

"Dad?" I tried.

My fingers fumbled for his pulse. I couldn't find it. Hurriedly, I lowered him to the floor and then braced my hands on his chest. My palms shoved down hard, over and over. I watched his face, hoping for any reaction.

None came.

Physicians appeared beside me. Guards pulled me away. Kyne and his assistants surrounded Dad till I couldn't see anything but his tail anymore.

It didn't move. Nothing changed. Kyne shouted orders, and I couldn't hear the words over the rushing in my ears.

I stared, trembling. I couldn't believe this. I just... It didn't make sense.

Dad was gone.

CHLOE

"So what's Kansas like?" Ina asked, hovering by a shelf near the ceiling of her spacious bedroom. She flipped open the lid to a stone box and glanced down to me curiously.

Sitting on the broad windowsill with plant leaves swaying behind me, I shrugged. "Flat, dry, though the western part is more like that than the eastern. My town is pretty small, so it's mostly just farmers who live there."

She returned her gaze to the box, and took out a pair of earrings. For a moment, she scrutinized them before finally raising them to her ear and studying her reflection in the mirror attached to the wall nearby. "What do you do for fun?"

I shrugged again. "Watch movies. Play video games. Hang out with friends."

"Huh. That ever get boring?"

"Sometimes, I guess."

She nodded thoughtfully and returned the earrings to the

box.

My brow furrowed. It'd been a few minutes since we arrived at her enormous apartment, but Ina showed no sign of having further plans. Idly drifting near the ceiling, she seemed more interested in investigating her jewelry.

And asking me random questions about where I'd come from.

"Anything else you want to know?" I hazarded.

She glanced to me again. Her face twisted with consternation, and then she folded the latest earrings in her hand and sank through the water to take a seat at my side.

"I just... we don't spend much time with them, you know? Humans. Oh, we hang out and have fun. But we don't *live* like them. It's just so odd to think about."

She shook her head like she was trying to wrap her mind around it, and then she exhaled, refocusing. "So tell me this. You said you never knew about the dehaian stuff till recently, right? So what's *that* like? Never changing like us? Always being in one form? How does that feel?"

I hesitated. "Normal."

She waited.

I wasn't sure how else to respond. "I mean, this isn't really an option, so..."

"It just seems like it'd be so *strange*. Like, sometimes I wonder how humans stand it, not being able to move around the ocean. Being stuck on land like that."

I shrugged.

She sighed. "Yeah. Normal." She shook her head again. "And *so* weird."

Drawing a breath, she turned her attention to the jewelry in her palm. Large emerald studs lay beside long ear cuffs of pale gold. Delicate chains looped down the length of the metal, with more emeralds in glistening settings running freely along them. Lifting one of the cuffs, she held it to my ear.

"Oh, yeah," she said. "You should definitely keep these. They'll look incredible on you."

I blinked. A smile twitched her lip as she put them in my hand.

"Up here, come on," she said, swimming toward the mirror above us.

Still feeling shocked, I followed.

"So, these are totally protected from water pressure here in Nyciena," Ina continued as I stopped in front of the mirror. "Just be careful not to take them outside the veil. They don't have any treatments on them like our supplies do, and they're too delicate for our natural magic to work on them either, so they–"

Her brow furrowed.

"What?" I asked. "What's wrong?"

She shook her head, looking uncertain. Turning, she swam out of the room.

I hesitated, and then set the earrings on the shelf. I followed her through the apartment and out through the leaves of the front door.

"Hey guys?" she called to the guards. "Is everything alright?"

The soldiers glanced at each other. "I believe so, your highness," one told her.

"Could you go make sure? I just–"

"Help!"

We froze, Zeke's cry echoing from a level above us. Shouting followed, and immediately two of the guards by Ina's apartment took off, racing for the upper floor.

I started after them, only to realize Ina wasn't with me. Looking back, I spotted her by the doorway, her face immobile with shock. The other guards hovered beside her, clearly torn between watching me and protecting their princess. For a heartbeat, Ina didn't move, and then suddenly she kicked hard in the water, shooting past me and up through the main corridor like a rocket.

Gasping, I chased her, the guards coming right behind.

The upper level of the palace was a zoo. Dehaians filled the hallway, and I could hear Zeke yelling at the end of it, his words lost in the din around me. At the archway, guards shouted orders to lock down the city, while servants cried out questions of what was going on.

I swam after the sound of Zeke's voice. People buffeted me, pushing by me in both directions, while others raced past overhead, following instructions all their own.

From a room at my side, Ren emerged into the chaos, and immediately I could tell something was wrong. His face was ashen, his eyes vacant, and he clutched his stomach like it pained him.

"Hey!" I yelled to the dehaians around me. "Hey, he needs help!"

I grabbed Ren's arms. His face tight, he looked at me, his hands still pressed to his middle.

"You..." he wheezed. "You did this..."

I stared as he doubled over and collapsed against the door-frame.

Guards appeared, shoving me aside as they tried to help him.

Ina screamed at the end of the hall.

I took off, pushing past people and trying to follow the sound. I could hear Physician Kyne ordering people back, and as I came closer, I saw Zeke, his arms wrapped around Ina as they both looked through a large doorway on the other side of the hall.

A guard blocked my path. "Stay back," he ordered.

"What happened?"

The man ignored me, his attention taken by others trying to get past. I turned back to Zeke.

He looked like he'd been hit with a two-by-four. One hand rubbing Ina's shoulder, he stared into the other room, his brow twitching down as though he was trying to make sense of what he saw.

Physician Kyne came through the door.

Silence fell and even the guards turned. I could feel the tension rise in the hall, like a collective breath suddenly being held.

"Is Prince Renekialen here?" he asked, his voice tightly controlled.

"H-he is ill too, sir," one of the guards answered. "Physicians are with him."

Kyne paused. He motioned the guard closer, and then whispered something to the man.

The guard's head shook in a jerky motion, and Kyne blinked. His gaze went to Zeke and Ina.

"I would speak with you both," he said.

A murmur ran through the hall as the two of them hesitated and then followed him into the room. The leaves of the door became like wood.

The murmuring grew louder. I heard Niall's name carried on the sound.

I looked around, realizing I hadn't seen him since the doctor had taken my blood a while ago. And he really should have been here.

Unless...

Heart pounding, I slipped past a group of servants whispering intently together and swam closer to the room, coming to a stop at the line of guards blocking the corridor.

Moments passed.

The leaves swayed as Kyne pushed by them and returned to the hallway.

"Their royal highnesses have retired to their chambers, pending further evaluation of the events today," he announced.

"Please return to your duties. We will provide additional information as it becomes available."

"What happened?" someone at the back of the crowd called. Shushing noises followed the sound.

Kyne's face tightened. "You have your orders."

He disappeared back through the leaves, which solidified like wood again the moment after he passed them.

The crowd began moving, meandering toward the arched exit at the end of the hallway and talking as they went. I hovered by the wall, forgotten for the moment.

I didn't know Zeke or Ina well, but it didn't take that to read their faces. Something horrible had happened. Truly, truly horrible.

And given where we were and how everyone was acting, I couldn't think of many scenarios beyond the most obvious.

Their father had been hurt.

Or worse.

I trailed the crowd back to the archway, and then swam downward, heading for my room. I wanted to find Zeke. To learn for certain what had occurred. But I didn't know where he stayed and I could guess at the odds of the guards letting me through to see him anyway.

Pushing past the leaves, I returned to my room. It couldn't be the Sylphaen. Regardless of what had happened, they couldn't have gotten past the guards to hurt the king this easily.

I hoped.

Instinctively, my hand went to the lighter patch on the stone doorframe, sealing up the leaves behind me. Swimming for the windows, I did the same to the plants there, turning to face the empty stillness of the room once I was done.

The Sylphaen couldn't be here. They just couldn't.

Unless there really *were* spies.

I shivered, eyeing the door and windows again. I hoped Zeke's dad was okay. That this was just some kind of mistake.

Though it'd have to be a mistake that had made Ren sick too. And that had kept Niall from coming when everyone else had.

I hovered in the middle of the room, uncertain what to do.

A knock at the door sent me jumping in the water. Heart pounding, I sank back down and then swam cautiously toward the noise. "Yes?"

"His highness wishes to speak with you," came a gruff voice.

I hesitated. "Which one?"

"Prince Zekerian."

My hand hit the patch on the doorframe. I pushed past the leaves. "What does he–"

There were half a dozen guards in the hall. And one of them held shackles.

I retreated, only to bump into the bare chest of another guard who had circled behind me. Grabbing my arms, the man shoved them forward while the other clapped the shackles on me so quickly, all I could do was gasp.

"You will come with us," the man behind me growled, his grip shifting to my shoulders. From the corner of my eye, I saw spikes emerge from his skin, the points dangerously close to my face and the implicit threat more than clear.

I swallowed. "Zeke sent you?" I asked, hoping desperately it wasn't true and that he didn't honestly think I had something to do with this.

Or that like the guy from the bookstore or the EMTs or all the other crazies who had tried to trap me in the past week alone, these guards weren't members of the Sylphaen too.

"Silence."

He pushed me forward, not letting go as I moved. The others fell in around me as I swam along the hall, and when we reached the archway and the open space beyond it, servants turned to stare. As he guided me downward, the guard's face could have been made from stone, but for the disgusted twitch his lip gave with every few seconds that passed by.

"I want to talk to Zeke," I said, looking from the guards to the motionless servants.

The guard released my shoulders to thumb a small stone clipped to his belt.

I shrieked as electricity shot through the shackles.

"Silence," he ordered.

Gasping, I stared at him, but he simply resumed his grip on my shoulders and shoved me forward.

We reached the ground floor and the men around me continued on, swimming away from the throne room. My eyes tracked across the water above us, hoping to find Zeke amid the countless dehaians floating there, but he was nowhere to be seen. Ina was likewise gone, and among the rest, I didn't recognize anyone at all.

The guards passed through the enormous castle doorway and out into the courtyard beyond. The veil parted ahead of us, allowing access to the city.

My gaze twitched to the larger veil in the distance. I didn't stand a chance of reaching it, not even if I managed to get away from the guards. They'd electrocute me before I swam a hundred feet.

And that was assuming I'd even know where to go once I was outside.

I shivered. The guards led me through the city to a smaller stone spire that stood alone on a span of sandy ground, isolated from the other buildings of town and lost on the outer fringes of Nyciena's lights. No plants blocked the entrance to this place. Instead, its only feature was a single gate of strangely shimmering metal at the spire's base. Guards surrounded it, though they moved aside when the soldiers with me drew nearer.

One of the men removed a stone from his belt and then approached the gate. The shimmering of the metal diminished, leaving only a hint of oily luminescence on the black surface of the bars.

He pushed on the gate and it swung back. The other guard thrust me ahead of him into the darkness.

"Keep moving," he muttered.

Trembling, I swam forward, my weird dehaian senses unable to find a floor in this place, and my eyes seeing nothing but a tunnel of rough stone in the shadows ahead of me.

Metal clanked. I spun. The men blocked any retreat to the closed gate, their bodies silhouetted by the dim light from the outside and their eyes gleaming in shades of green and brown.

"I said keep moving," the nearest guard growled.

"Where?"

His hand twitched to the stone on his belt. I flinched back, watching him.

"Move."

Fear and disbelief bubbled up in me, but I turned, swimming into the shadows and trying to trust every other sense I had to tell me what was below.

"Go down," the guard ordered.

Swallowing hard, I swam down. On the walls, I began to sense openings, though quivering feelings blocked them and sent shivers through the water around me. Whispers twisted through the darkness, emanating from beyond the strange vibrations and murmuring words I couldn't understand. I bit my lip, fighting not to draw their attention with any sound.

"Sexy…"

I gasped, jerking away from the lascivious whisper at my side. Yellow-green eyes glinted in the darkness.

"Come closer, sexy girl…"

"Shut it," a guard snarled.

A clang echoed through the shadows, followed by a retreating growl.

"Go," the guard told me.

My heart pounding enough to choke me, I looked to the water behind me. With everything in me, I wanted to flee back toward the distant light of the outside world. But the shackles still held my forearms and, again, I knew how that would go.

Trying to ignore the inarticulate whispers still coming from the darkness nearby, I did as the guard ordered.

Seconds crept past, each one a frightening eternity all its own. The ceiling sloped, tracking us as we swam downward. The dim glow of light from the world above gradually melted away, till even my glowing eyes couldn't make anything of the black around us, rendering me truly blind. The whispers faded the deeper we swam, until only silence remained.

"Here," the guard growled.

I jumped at the sudden sound, and heard one of the others scoff, his senses picking out the frightened motion where his eyes could not. Swimming past me in the darkness, a guard did something to a quivering space on the wall at my side.

The quivering feeling dissipated, and then a door-like shape moved back, making a metallic scraping noise as it went. I swallowed.

"In."

"Why are you—"

My shriek cut through the blackness, and somewhere

overhead, shouts and howls broke out.

"Quiet!" one of the guards bellowed.

The noises diminished.

Tears choked me. I hovered in the water, shaking with the desire to just swim for the exit I knew was somewhere above me, past the black.

"In," the guard repeated.

I shivered.

And I felt his hand moving toward his belt again.

I retreated through the opening.

"Hands out," he said.

I extended my arms. The shackles dropped away.

"Don't move," the guard ordered as he swam back through the opening, the other guards hovering outside it.

Metal scraped over stone. A clank rang out, and then the water trembled as the quivering feeling returned.

The guards left.

A soft gasp escaped me. I could feel that walls surrounded me, only a few feet away on any side, with the floor and ceiling the same. Shaking, I inched toward the strange quiver in the water ahead. My hands reached out, my senses guiding me in the utter darkness.

Sparks bit my fingertips and sent a crackle of electricity through my arms. Choking on a cry, I jerked back.

A prison cell. They'd locked me in a prison cell.

Trembling, I hovered in the darkness, my tail moving to keep me afloat. Ren had blamed me for whatever had made him sick. And the guards had heard him. They'd been right there when he'd said this was all my fault.

Distant moans carried through the blackness beyond the cell. I drew an unsteady breath.

So this was Ren. His doing. Probably, anyway. And Zeke... Zeke would find out about it. Or Niall. Or Ina. But regardless, someone would come for me. They'd get me out of here.

Unless it *was* actually the Sylphaen and they were heading this way right now.

I closed my eyes, fighting back a surge of panic. It wasn't. I was fine. Sure, it was dark. Cold. Filled with whispers and God knew what else down here in the black, but I was dehaian. Half-landwalker too, and till a few weeks ago I hadn't known either existed, but that wasn't the point. I *was* dehaian. I didn't need light to know what was around me. I didn't need any-thing. So I wasn't going to freak out about this. I'd survived changing, survived the neiphiandine.

For that matter, I'd survived a run-in with the Sylphaen barely twenty-four hours ago.

I'd survive this.

And somehow, some way, I wouldn't be down here for long.

ZEKE

Ina hadn't stopped crying since the soldiers escorted us back to my apartment. Her quiet sobs formed an undercurrent to the senseless words that everyone kept insisting upon saying. Guards and physicians swirled around the room, blurring into one another while they checked and confirmed and asked things about which I couldn't find it in myself to care.

Because Dad was dead.

And I didn't know how to wrap my mind around that.

He'd always been here, a part of our lives even if the times we actually saw him were rare. He was our king as much as our father, after all, and it wasn't like we could ever really get close to him as a result. But he'd still been here. Constant. A shape defining the world we lived in.

And now he was gone.

On autopilot, I nodded to something Orvien had said, and then looked away as the old chamberlain swam off. He could handle this. The servants and the questions. I didn't need to tell him what to do. That wasn't my job.

At least, it hadn't been.

A breath pressed from my chest. Ren was sick too. He was laid up in his rooms, where Kyne was trying to keep him stable. As for Niall, he'd been found in his own apartment, collapsed on the floor, unconscious but alive.

There was only one conclusion. Only one thing on everyone's mind.

Someone had tried to kill my family. They'd gotten past every soldier, every checkpoint, and all manner of protections, and they'd tried to kill my family. Somehow, they'd missed Ina and me, though from the guards surrounding the room, palace security wasn't taking any chances that the assassins wouldn't try again.

I'd worried at first that it was the Sylphaen, except that made little sense. Why go after Dad and not Chloe? Why try to kill half the royal family and leave her alone?

Besides, it wasn't like we didn't have enough enemies, even without counting the Sylphaen.

Kyne said it had been poison. It had to be. Dad had no injuries, short of the blackish discoloration of his lips and the horrible way the blood vessels in his eyes and skin had broken.

I didn't think I'd ever be able to forget that.

"Your highness?"

I blinked, looking up at the dark-haired and bronze-scaled guard. Tiberion, I thought his name was. One of Ren's commanders.

"What?" I asked vaguely.

"Captain Renekialen is awake."

Ina surged up from the seat. "He's okay? Is he–"

"It was close, but the physician thinks he will recover, yes," Tiberion answered.

She was already heading for the door.

I swam after her, Tiberion coming behind and ordering the others to follow.

"Niall?" I asked the commander.

"Still unconscious, highness. Physician Liana remains with him."

I exhaled, fighting to appear calm as I slid past the plants into the hall. Up ahead, a dozen soldiers chased Ina, each of them struggling to stay with her as she raced onward.

She was already at Ren's bedside by the time I reached his rooms.

"I'm fine, Ina," he assured her, his hoarse voice belying the words. Strain showed on his bloodless face as he pushed away from the sand-bed. With his free hand, he patted her fingers, which were clutching his own.

Then his gaze found me by the door.

Anger drove everything else from his expression.

"Get out," he growled.

My chest tightened, fury making it hard to breathe. Dad was dead. If he didn't wake up soon, Niall might be too. And Ren had the audacity – the sheer, pigheaded *audacity* – to try to take that out on me.

"Ren," Ina tried.

"Stay out of this, Ina," he ordered, his voice rough. He looked back to me. "I said get the hell–"

"Why?" I demanded. "So you can pretend this is *my* fault? That it has something to do with… with *what*? The parties I have? The girls I've slept with? Something *else* about me you don't fucking *approve* of?" A scoff escaped me, painful in its strength. "God *damn* you, Ren, I was there when Dad *died*! I was *right there* when the poison–"

Ina gave a choked sob, and I cut off, shaking. "I did everything I could to save him," I continued, my voice tight. "I tried–"

"Save it," Ren snapped. "You're the reason he's dead."

I stared, speechless.

"Ren," Ina protested, "you don't mean–"

"You brought that spy here," he continued over her. "You gave her access to Dad, me, everyone. You insisted she stay, when I told you–"

"It wasn't *Chloe*!" I shouted. "Dammit, it *couldn't* have been. She never went *near* Dad, except for the time *you* hauled her into the throne room in chains! She's hardly even been out of my sight since–"

"I'm sure."

I choked on a breath, shaking with the urge to slam a fist into his condescending face.

"Spies don't have to work alone, brother," Ren said. "So rest assured, we're going to interview every servant and courtier on the premises to learn which ones are her allies. And in the meantime, I've made certain your stupidity won't harm the only sister we have left."

I froze. A shiver built in my stomach, rippling outward. "What have you done?" I whispered, afraid to know.

"What you should have."

The trembling grew stronger.

Ina's brow twitched down warily. "Ren, where's Chloe?"

He glanced to her, saying nothing.

Ina's gaze slid to me, fear in her eyes, and she pulled her fingers from beneath Ren's own. "You didn't hurt her... right?"

"I've only put her where she can't do any more damage," he told her.

"*Where?*"

The word came out hot and savage, and Ren paused, regarding me for a moment before he responded to it.

"As the new king of Yvaria – no thanks to you – I'm going to say that's no longer your concern."

I surged forward. "Where *is* she, you pompous son of a–"

Guards circled in front of me, blocking my path. Past their shoulders, I stared at him.

"Commander Tiberion," Ren called. "Have your people escort my brother back to his apartment and keep him there."

"If you've hurt her..." I threatened.

"That will be all," Ren replied, glancing to Tiberion.

The guards moved forward, crowding me back with their

presence, and for a moment, it was all I could do not to shove past them, just to pound that damn supercilious look off his face.

"Your highness," Tiberion said beside me, the warning in his voice clear.

I looked from my brother to the commander, while in front of me, the guards showed edges of spikes on their arms, ready to defend their king.

There wasn't a hope of getting past them.

And trying would only give Ren the satisfaction of watching his soldiers muscle me out of his presence.

Furious, I spun and swam from the room.

Guards trailed me all the way back to my apartment, and when we reached it, they took up stations around the door and beyond the windows.

And then they sealed them both.

Fighting not to give into the urge to break something, I hovered in the center of the room, my tail kicking every few moments to keep me from sinking to the floor.

I couldn't believe this. Ren. He'd postponed having Tiberion tell us he was awake till after he'd taken Chloe away. Till he'd gotten the guards on the same page, and probably the servants too.

Us. His own family, who'd worried he might be dying.

My tail kicked again, propelling me back up into the center of the room as I stared at the door. In the back of my mind, I'd always dreaded what would happen when he took the throne. Whether he'd order me off to supervise some remote province on the edge of the northern wastes, or just keep me here under his thumb for the rest of my life. I'd hoped Dad would never abdicate, and maybe live forever at the same time. I'd dreamed of him seeing Ren for the jerk he was, and passing him over for Niall instead.

But I'd never wanted to imagine this. Dad dead. Niall possibly the same. And this girl I'd just been trying to help, now lost who knew where, if she was even still alive.

I closed my eyes. Niall had Liana, one of the best physicians in Nyciena, looking after him. I'd find Chloe, and she'd be fine as well. And as for the bastards who'd attacked my family...

Opening my eyes, I looked from the door to the windows. There had to be a way out of here.

The fejeria blocking the door whispered as they loosened back to passable leaves.

"Thanks, guys," Ina called to the guards.

The smile on her face vanished the moment she slid into the room. "Are you okay?" she asked as she pressed a hand to the doorframe without looking at it, sealing up the fejeria again.

"Where's Chloe? Did Ren say anything to you about–"

I cut off, grimacing as she shook her head.

Ina hesitated. "Zeke, do you think there's a *chance* she did–"

"No."

The answer came out harsher than I intended and my grimace returned. "It's not possible, Ina," I amended more gently. "I mean, that thing she does to the water? The Sylphaen, the neiphiandine, and the fact those bastards nearly killed her twice?" I shook my head. "If that was all just a trick to get close enough to poison Dad, it's got to be the most complicated con game in history."

Ina nodded reluctantly. "Ren just–"

"Ren's obsessed with the idea she's a spy."

"He just wants to find who tried to hurt us."

I looked away.

"Who did this, Zeke?"

Her voice was small, the way it'd been when we were kids and she would come to my room after she'd had a nightmare.

I swam over and put my arms around her. She hugged me tightly, her fingers gripping my back. A choked sob escaped her.

"I don't know," I admitted. "But we'll figure it out."

And then they'd pay.

I didn't add the words, knowing they would just upset her more. After what happened with Miri, revenge was something of a sore topic for us all.

No matter how much I wanted it right now.

I drew a breath, pushing the thought away as Ina nodded into my shoulder.

A moment passed. She leaned back from me, sniffling a bit as she tried to return her ordinarily confident expression to her face.

"Ren'll make a good king," she said, and from her tone I couldn't tell if she was working to convince me or herself.

I didn't respond, not wanting to argue. She seemed to read into the silence anyway.

"Just give him time to calm down," she urged. "He's shaken by this too."

I grimaced. "I can't. I need to find Chloe. Find out what he's done."

She hesitated. "I really don't think he'd hurt her, even if he does think she's a spy."

I looked at Ina. She dropped her gaze to the floor.

"Can you help me?" I asked.

"I'm sure he's ordered the guards not to say anything. And if you do this, now that he's king it'll be–"

"Can you help me?" I repeated, not wanting to hear it. I knew what I was asking would mean. Treason. Betraying an order of the king. And worse, aiding the person that king said had helped kill our dad. He wouldn't hurt Ina for it; he had a soft spot for her just as he'd had for Miri. But me...

I'd be lucky if I ended up on the border of the northern wastes. More likely, I'd spend the rest of my life in prison.

But I couldn't let a girl I'd brought all this way into the ocean just disappear. I couldn't simply forget that. Not after how much I'd tried to help her, and not with the people chasing her still lurking around. With everything in me, I wanted to be out there right now, hunting down whoever had dared to hurt our family.

I just had to do this too.

"Ina?" I pressed.

She glanced up, hesitance obvious in her expression. "I don't know, Zeke. I mean, Ren's not a monster. Really. And we need you here. With Niall hurt and Dad..." She shook her head. "We *need* you. I know Chloe's nice – or she seemed to be, at least – but if you help her..."

"I can't let her get caught up in this, Ina. You *saw* Ren. Monster or not, he wants somebody to blame. And it wasn't her. It was someone, and I'm going to do everything I can to help us find out who... but first I need to make sure Ren doesn't hurt the wrong person."

She looked back down. "I don't want you to leave," she whispered. "Please."

I wrapped her hand in my own. This was the side of Ina she almost never showed. The one behind all the devil-may-care confidence and flirting.

The one that had lost too much of our family already.

"I'll be careful," I promised. "And I won't be gone long. I'm just going to get Chloe away from the city. Find her someplace safe to hide till we figure out who really did this. And then I'll be back, okay?"

Trembling, she nodded. Pushing the fear from her expression, she looked up at me again. "I'm holding you to that."

My lip twitched. "So does that mean you'll help?"

Ina sighed. "Yeah, alright." Her gaze went to the door, and she drew another breath, her typical self-assurance creeping back onto her face. "I'll just go, uh, talk to the guards."

I smiled.

10

CHLOE

Days had passed. Or minutes. In the pitch-black water, my pounding heart made the only sound, sparing the occasional whispers and mutters from the prisoners somewhere above me.

And otherwise, nothing changed.

Floating in the middle of the tiny cell, I took another steadying breath, focusing on keeping myself from surrendering to panic. Earlier, I'd searched the walls, hoping for a crack, a drain, anything to give me a chance of getting out. But the walls, ceiling and floor were solid. Only a soft, slimy fuzz grew over them, thick enough to make it seem as though they'd been undisturbed for years. I'd even tried the door again, zapping myself on it so many times I'd begun to feel like an experiment subject who couldn't figure out what she wasn't supposed to touch.

But it didn't matter, I reminded myself. Someone would

come. Someone would find me here. Ren couldn't get away with this forever.

The still water stirred beyond my cell.

I froze, my skin prickling at the faint current. My heart picked up speed as the motion grew stronger and then came to a stop in a blur of quivering water beyond the cell door.

Four pairs of glowing eyes watched me.

And their owners didn't say a word.

"Hello?" I whispered.

No one replied. Like a flicked-off light switch, the quivering feeling that guarded the door disappeared, and then the shape of the dehaians became clear. Three men, with a woman between them.

Metal scraped on stone. The three men swam into the cell. I retreated, spikes growing on my arms as the trio fanned out, blocking any hope of getting past them.

"Who are you?" I demanded. "What do you–"

My back bumped into the wall. The dehaians swam at me. Two grabbed my arms, avoiding the spikes, while the other snagged my hair and yanked my head backward, making me shout in pain.

A black shape enveloped my face. My head. A click sounded by my ear as I struggled in their grasp, and then a numbing feeling spread down my body, making the water like dense gel.

I gasped and choked on the sludge the ocean had become.

A blindfold. They'd put me in one of those blindfold

things, just like Ren had done.

I twisted, trying to break their grip as I fought to tear the muffling fabric from my head.

Something slammed into my face, knocking me sideways and sending the muddy world spinning. My ears rang like a gong in the silence of the blindfold, and then another blow came to the insides of my elbows.

Tingles shot through my arms, and the spikes retreated like a reflex. Shackles clamped down on my forearms, and then jerked forward, as though they were connected to a leash.

I pulled back, fighting them.

A fist punched my stomach, doubling me over, and then hit my back, propelling me down. Electricity found me before the floor did, shooting through the shackles and sending me thrashing. I screamed, trying to escape the pain, and another fist struck me, driving me hard into the slimy ground and then returning with a second blow to my face just to make sure I got the point.

The shackles lurched forward again, hauling me up. The dehaians dragged me through the water.

Tears choked me. Everything hurt. My face, my stomach, my arms, even the water that slid into my nose and mouth like a dense, burning goo. I could taste blood amid the saltwater in my mouth, but I couldn't tell if anything was broken. The sense of wrongness screaming through my mind from the blindfold blocked everything but the generalized blur of pain.

If I ever made it back to land, I'd never leave again.

The thought hurt as much as anything else. I couldn't understand this. What had happened. I didn't want this. Life had been normal a few weeks ago. True, my parents were crazy – and sort of not my parents – but otherwise it'd been fine. And now I was here. Being beaten up. Pulled through the water like a fish on a line. It hurt, all of it did. I didn't want people to hurt me anymore.

I just wanted to go home.

The dehaians slowed. I trembled, wanting to fight, not wanting them to hit me again.

"Prisoner transfer," came a woman's voice, the sound murky to my ears.

Someone answered, though their words were too muddled by the hood for me to understand.

"I am aware of what you were told, but I have orders to inspect her condition before transfer, and I can't do that in the pit, now can I?"

The mumble returned, terse and official-sounding.

"Good," the woman replied.

The shackles jerked forward again. Gel-like water slid over my skin, the pressure changing infinitesimally as the dehaians turned at corners or pulled me onward faster.

"Stop," the woman ordered.

The dehaians did as commanded. Shivering, I strained to hear or feel anything of my surroundings.

"Keep watch," she said, and the sludge moved a bit as one of them swam away. "Put her in."

Hands grabbed my shoulders, shoving me downward. Panic made me struggle, but a fist followed immediately. Choking, I doubled over again.

The dehaians grabbed my tail, bending it sharply. They pushed me down, and hard surfaces contacted my scales and my back, and then met my side as well.

Something clunked above me. Curled into a ball with my tail crushed to my chest and my fin twisted beneath me, I tried to straighten, only to find that walls surrounded me.

A box. I was in a box.

My heart began pounding harder as I shoved against the immovable sides. A cry escaped me, the sound somewhere between a sob and a scream.

A thud echoed through the box, and then the shackles sent a jolt of electricity through me. I shrieked, trying to retreat with nowhere to go.

"Silence," one of the men growled.

Trembling, I choked on another sob as the charge faded away.

I wanted to go home. Oh God, I just wanted to get out of here and go home.

"You have the neiphiandine blend ready?" the woman asked.

A muffled response came.

"Good. Inject her again when we arrive. No telling what

might happen if that first dose wears off."

They lifted the box. It rocked as they swam, pressing me to one wall and then the next. I couldn't tell when we went up or down, or gain any hint of where we were, and when they finally slowed, I was shaking so hard, I could barely breathe.

"Medical supplies," the woman said. "Very volatile."

Muddled words.

"Thank you."

The box jostled as they started moving again.

Minutes crept past. My air came in short gasps, and in my mind, I kept repeating Niall's words from a million years before. I could breathe. No matter what it felt like, I could still breathe.

And somehow, I'd get out of this.

Biting back another sob before it could escape, I fought to make myself believe the words. I didn't know how I was going to do it, but I would. I'd get out of here. I *would*.

A muffled sound came from beyond the walls, and the box lurched as the dehaians stopped. In the darkness of the hood, I looked up, my heart pounding.

"Excuse me?" the woman demanded.

The muffled words repeated.

"These are medical supplies, transported by the order of the king. How dare you—"

The voice interrupted her, the tone intense.

"You decrepit old toad, I will not—"

Someone shouted and the box fell. Gravity and water

fought as the box and I dropped, and when the ground came, everything went sideways and then tumbled end over end. Landing finally with my fin above me and my back pressed hard to the wall, I lay there, wanting to scream and too terrified to make a sound.

Trembling, I pushed my shackled hands against the lid. Nothing moved. I could be on a cliff. Pressed against a wall. Anywhere.

I gasped, and then risked shoving harder.

Everything toppled.

I cried out, but the box just stopped, coming to rest right way up. Shaking hard, I shoved at the lid, but nothing changed.

Scraping sounded on the walls, followed by a shift in the pressure of the water, and then I heard a muffled voice above me.

"What the hell?"

The numbing hood vanished, and the ocean filled the void in a crescendo of pain. Every rock and current for hundreds of yards around appeared in my head, while bruises made themselves known so suddenly, it felt like I was being hit all over again. Shrieking at the sudden cacophony of sensation, I cringed tighter into a ball.

A hand reached down, wrapping around my shoulder and without even thinking, I fought against it, struggling away and managing to swim a few yards before pain made me falter and sink to the seafloor.

"Hey," came a voice. "Hey now. Chloe, wait."

I gasped, looking back.

Zeke's grandfather hovered by the box, his expression a mix of incredulity and shock. In his hand, he held a torch, while a stone-like gun hung from the belt at his waist. We were on a rocky slope, with the water beyond the blue flames nearly black and the other dehaians nowhere to be seen.

Breathless, I stared at him, trying to form words though I didn't know what I hoped to say.

He pushed away from the box and came toward me. I flinched back. He stopped.

"What were you doing in there?" he asked.

I shook my head and then winced, my ears ringing with the motion. My face took the opportunity to protest next, broadcasting the fact my left eyelid and cheek were rapidly swelling and couldn't take many more attempts at expression.

"I'm not going to hurt you," he continued carefully.

I didn't move, uncertain whether to trust the words. Zeke didn't like him. From the sound of it, neither did anyone short of Ina. For that matter, he'd come close to threatening me the last time we met.

And now, inexplicably, he was here.

"How did you... why are you..."

He paused, watching me. "My son was killed."

I stared at him, torn between horror that the king was dead and thoughts of Zeke and Ina. Of the looks on their faces, when I'd seen them in the hall. Of the pain they must be going through.

Of the fact the guards said Zeke wanted to speak to me, right before they'd arrested me.

I blinked, my gaze falling to the seafloor. Surely he hadn't *actually* been the one to do that. It must have been Ren.

Although, now that I thought about it, I'd seen Ren. He'd been hurt too. He'd fallen over with me right there next to him, and if whatever had caused that had killed him too...

I felt sick.

"Do they... do they know who did it?" I asked, pushing the words past my nausea as I looked back up at the old man.

His brow drawing down, he regarded me for a moment, as if reading something in my expression. "Not yet. Rumor in the city is the guards are looking for the one who poisoned him, but so far, they haven't found anyone." He paused. "Some of the mercenary factions used to use this trick, though. Smuggling people around in boxes, though it's pretty hard on the ones inside. And when I saw that group leaving the capital with a container of medical supplies, I thought perhaps they were trying to sneak the killer out."

He looked me over again. "I didn't expect to find you."

Panic hit me, making me want to bolt. He couldn't think I'd done this. He couldn't...

"Chloe, it's alright," he told me. "Assassins aren't typically given shackles and blindfolds and beaten to within an inch of being ground meat. Especially not successful ones."

I shivered. I didn't want to think about what I looked like. The fact that it hurt when I breathed and the left side of my face had swelled so much it was becoming hard to see was horrible enough.

Jirral moved away from the box, not taking his eyes from me. "How about we get those things off of you?"

I tensed, but didn't retreat as he came close and then set the torch aside. Still watching me, he reached into the small satchel on his belt and drew out a metal clip that shimmered with blue light. Taking my hands, he turned them so the underside of the shackles came into view.

"This is something I picked up in the Prijoran Zone," he explained as he stuck the clip into the lock. Studying his own work intently, he pulled the small bit of metal around, twisting it first one way then the other and watching while it shifted from pale to darker blue. "Folks there don't take too kindly to chains. They like to have ways of getting their friends out, if the need arises."

The clip became deep blue and something clicked. The shackles popped open.

"There we go," he said, tossing the restraints away and then retrieving his torch.

I rubbed my forearms. "Thank you."

He nodded. "Come on." He motioned to the slope. "The cold's going to start getting to you if you stay down here too long."

I pushed up from the ground and then gasped as pain lanced through my side. He reached out to take my arm as I sank again. I flinched back.

126

"Hey," he urged, holding his hands up. "I promise, I won't hurt you. But you need help."

Trembling, I watched him, and then gave a small nod.

"Just keep breathing and take it slow," he said. Gently, he pulled me away from the rocky seafloor, pausing every time I tensed.

At a pace that would have been dwarfed by a sloth, we swam up the slope.

"Where are the others?" I asked.

"The ones who had you in there?"

I nodded.

"Two of them swam off. The ones holding onto the box..." He paused. "They're down below us. They won't be coming back."

A breath escaped me as my eyes flicked to the weapon on his belt.

"Can you tell me what happened?" he asked.

"I think they were Sylphaen," I told him, my voice small.

"Seems a safe guess, given what Zeke said."

I managed another nod. "They came to my cell–"

"Cell?" he repeated, slowing to a stop. "Why were you in a cell?"

Fear rose. He was going to think I'd done something to deserve this. He was going to–

"Chloe?"

"It wasn't my fault," I pled, tears rising at the thought that, like his son and grandson, he'd decide I was in Nyciena to hurt people. "I'm not a spy. I *swear* I'm not. Ren locked me up. His soldiers did. They thought I was, but I'm not. I just came here to get the neiphian… the neiphi…"

My head spun and I drifted sideways, sinking to the ground.

"Hey!" He grabbed me. "Breathe, Chloe. Please. It's okay. Breathe."

I tried to do as he said.

"So neiphiandine," he prompted. "That's what you were trying to say?"

"I'm not a spy," I whispered.

"Okay," he agreed.

I nodded, clinging to the word. "The Sylphaen gave it to me. They made me change, but I got away from them. Zeke brought me here. He said the doctors could fix it. But Ren…"

"He locked you up?"

"I think so. I don't know. When their dad… I thought he was just sick. I knew something was wrong, but I didn't think… and then guards came to my room and told me Zeke wanted to talk, but…"

Jirral's mouth tightened.

"They put me in a cell. And later, those other people came."

"And they did this to you?"

"I tried to fight them."

He let out a breath. A moment passed, and then he drew me away from the seafloor again. "Come on."

The darkness lessened as we continued upward, and when

we crested the top of the slope, I could feel a jumble of rocks in the distance, the shape roughly like a line. Stone spires twisted up from the seafloor beyond the array, and through the twilit water, I could just sense the ghostly form of a mountain.

But they were all lifeless. Motionless amid the ocean's current.

"Is that Nyciena?"

He gave me a curious look.

"I didn't see it," I tried to explain. "Ren had me blindfolded."

Jirral paused. "Yes, that's Nyciena. From the other side of the veil, anyway."

He looked to the ocean behind us, his face tightening as though he was wrestling with a decision. "This way," he said finally.

Drawing me with him, he swam out across the valley and away from the invisible veil.

"Where are we going?" I asked.

"To my camp. They'll learn you're gone eventually, and given how things have been so far, it'd be better if you weren't in the city when that happens."

I hesitated. "You have a camp out here? What about your house?"

"That was just a place I rented. I'm not too popular with the family, as I'm sure you noticed, and sometimes courtiers or guards think they'll take advantage of that. Gain favor with

Torvias by confiscating my things and throwing me out of town. I've found it's useful to have somewhere to go if that happens." He paused, regret furrowing his brow. "Or at least they used to. Maybe with Ren, things will be different."

"Ren's alive?"

He nodded. "Sick but alive, yes."

I didn't say anything, relieved that Zeke maybe hadn't been the one to order me into a cell after all. We continued on until the hills I'd felt when I'd first approached Nyciena came into view.

"Up here," he said, leading me around the hill and up toward a cave I could sense high on the side.

The pale blue light of the torch caught on the outline of the cave opening when we came close, and inside, nothing was waiting but a small bag of supplies and a pile of dark green seaweed I could only assume was a bed. Jagged bits of quartz formed much of the ceiling and reflected the torchlight, brightening the space.

As we came through the opening, Jirral set the torch aside and then helped me toward the bed. The seaweed gave beneath me like a soft mattress, and I could feel exhaustion drag me deeper into it as I sat down. Leaving me for a moment, he swam back to the bag by the opposite wall.

"I'm going to give you some sieranchine," he told me. "It should help heal what they did to you."

My brow twitched down at the word. It sounded familiar, like the same thing Zeke had used on me a million years and one week ago when I'd been in the hospital.

I shivered, not wanting to remember the other times the Sylphaen had attacked me.

Jirral took out a container and then returned to the bedside, removing the top as he went. With a bit of the seaweed torn from the leaves below me, he scooped out a handful of shimmering clear gel.

"This won't hurt," he assured me.

He reached out, gently putting the gel to the side of my face. I gasped as tingles spread through my skin.

But then they faded. And so did the pain.

I looked up at him as the vision in my left eye began to clear.

"Here," he said, extending the seaweed and medicine to me. "Put this where it hurts on the rest of you, okay?"

Nodding, I took the container and then carefully scooped out some of the medicine. The gel glittered like particles of light were trapped within it. Gingerly, I pressed it to my side. More tingles rushed through my chest, bringing a surge of energy with them and driving my exhaustion back. The gel seemed to absorb almost instantly into my scales, as if soaked up by a sponge, and as it did, the pain that had stabbed me with every deep breath just melted into a faint throb.

Another application did the same to my aching midsection, where the dehaians had punched me over and over again.

"Not too much," he cautioned as I went to remove another dose from the jar.

I hesitated, and then handed the container to him. He returned the lid to its top, and then swam back to his bag.

"What was that? The see..." I faltered, unsure how to pronounce the word, and then regrouped, "the stuff you just gave me."

His brow furrowed as he looked at me again. "Sieranchine? It's medical gel infused with magic by physician's alchemy."

I tensed at the curiosity in his tone. Like any dehaian would have known that, and he couldn't figure out why I hadn't. "Oh."

Jirral paused, his questioning expression deepening. "Chloe, why are the Sylphaen after you?"

I dropped my gaze from his. I didn't know what to say to him. How much to trust him. Zeke hadn't told him hardly anything when last they'd met, and there had to be a reason.

But he'd also saved me. Maybe not intentionally, but he could have just left me out there once he'd discovered I was the one in that box. And instead, he'd helped me and treated what those people had done.

That had to be worth something.

"I'm not sure," I said.

Annoyance tinged his face.

"I'm not," I insisted. "At least, not about all of their reasons. But I think I know why they hate me."

His brow drew down.

"I'm... I'm not fully dehaian. I'm half landwalker."

His curiosity turned to surprise as his brow climbed. "Half

landwalker."

I nodded. "My mom. She died when I was born."

Jirral's gaze moved over me like he couldn't believe what he saw. "I didn't think landwalkers existed anymore. If they ever had at all."

I didn't know how to respond.

"And the legends of their children with dehaians… How did your father help you survive?"

"My father didn't raise me. I've never met him. I grew up in Kansas. It's one of the–"

"One of the middle states. I know."

He sounded shocked. Distracted. Like he was still working to process what he was hearing.

I took a breath. "I'd never come near the ocean in my life. My parents – I mean, they're not really. I-I found out I was adopted just… just yesterday." I struggled to regroup, trying not to think about the whirlwind my life had become. "But they're landwalkers. Both of them. They kept me away from everything to do with the ocean."

"And the Sylphaen?"

I gave an awkward shrug. "Found me when I came to Santa Lucina. I'd snuck out with a friend, and Mom and Dad–" I grimaced, hating how I couldn't figure out what I was supposed to call them, "they didn't know till after I left. But the Sylphaen started trying to catch me by the second day I was there." My skin crawled. "Zeke said they even drowned a few girls just to find out which one was me."

Jirral looked away.

I watched him, trying to read his silence. "Do you know why they want to hurt me, Jirral?"

For a moment, he didn't respond. "Well, they're obsessed with their idea of purity."

My gaze turned to the opening of the cave. It could just be that, except it seemed like more. From everything Marty and Colin, the EMTs who'd attacked me in the ambulance, had said... it just seemed like more than that.

"And then there's the odd thing you do to the water."

I glanced back at him.

"It changes," he said. "It's even less now than when I first saw you with Zeke and Ina. Practically nonexistent. Are you controlling it?"

I shook my head nervously. "I don't even know what you're talking about. I don't feel anything."

He sighed.

A moment passed. I looked to the cave opening. My face didn't hurt as much anymore, and neither did my sides. I wasn't back to a hundred percent – and until the neiphiandine got out of my system, I didn't think I would be – but I was better.

And now I just wanted to go home, wherever that was.

"Will this medicine help with neiphiandine?" I asked Jirral.

He hesitated, obviously hearing the hope in my voice.

"Probably not," he admitted. "Neiphiandine was designed to stay in someone's system even when they're on other medications."

A breath escaped me. I looked back to the open water.

"Listen," Jirral said. "I need to head into Nyciena. See if my grandkids are still alright, and if anything's changed. I'll be back soon."

Alarmed, I turned to him.

"You'll be fine," he assured me. "No one comes this way."

I didn't respond, hoping he was right.

"Chloe," he said, swimming closer. "You'll be *fine*. But Zeke... that boy really cares about you. He would never have come with you to see me if he didn't."

My brow twitched down, but Jirral just continued, "If he finds out that you're missing, though, I don't want him to worry or do anything stupid. And I need to know that he and his siblings are safe." He put a hand to my shoulder. "I'll leave the torch. This'll only take me a little bit."

Worry bubbling up inside, I managed a nod, though the motion wasn't anywhere near the truth. I didn't want to be alone out here. Out where the Sylphaen might find me.

He gave me a sympathetic smile, and then handed me the torch. "It'll just be a little bit," he repeated.

And then he swam out of the cave.

My fingers wrapped around the torch's base, the narrow pillar of stone cold in my hands despite the impossible blue fire flickering from its top. I drew my tail up close to my chest, my eyes locked on the cave opening.

I'd wait. Give him a little while like he asked. I needed his help to figure out which direction it was to Santa Lucina anyway.

But I wouldn't stay here forever. No matter what Jirral and everyone else seemed to think of Zeke's feelings – of which I'd swear he'd never shown the slightest hint that *I* could see – I was done with Nyciena and this world. The Sylphaen were here, along with Ren and who knew what other dangers.

Neiphiandine or no neiphiandine, I was going back to Santa Lucina at the first chance I got.

11

ZEKE

I'd swum the length of the room a thousand times before Ina returned.

And the moment she came through the door, I could tell the news wasn't good.

"What happened?" I asked, my heart climbing my throat.

Ina sealed the fejeria behind her, not meeting my eyes. "Ren had the guards lock her in the pit. But, um…"

"*But?*" I repeated, swimming closer.

"Physician Liana took her back out. Had her blindfolded and cuffed, and said she had orders to inspect Chloe's health before a prisoner transfer." She hesitated. "The castle guards haven't seen her or Chloe since. Ren's ordered a search of the city to find them."

A breath escaped me.

"Liana didn't even *try* taking care of Niall," Ina continued desperately. "She just left him lying unconscious in his bed the moment no one was watching. The guys at the pit said she had a few guards with her, but... Zeke, you don't think Liana's behind what happened to Dad, do you? I mean, she's been a palace physician for years. How could she just...?"

My heart pounding, I gave Ina a dark look, knowing I couldn't allay her fears. "Where did they last see Chloe?"

"At the pit entrance by the castle gate, but–"

I swam for the window.

"Zeke, please! If Liana's–"

The fejeria scraped my scales as I shoved through before the opening command took full effect. I ignored it. Shooting past the guards, I raced for the veil surrounding the palace.

That bastard had her put into the pit. Down in the dark with the criminals and psychopaths awaiting transport to the prisons along the borders. And now...

Liana. Second only to Kyne. Nearly as trusted by the king as we were.

And, with Chloe as her second target, most likely a Sylphaen.

I could hear people shouting behind me, calling for me to stop.

If I got my hands on that woman...

Up ahead, a few of the guards moved to intercept me as I swam for the veil, but at the sight of the spikes on my arms, they pulled back.

My lip twitched. I sped through the barrier and magic sizzled over me as I passed.

I veered left on the other side of the veil. The castle wall fell behind me, and then half the city did too, and when I finally neared the pit, I could see Tiberion at the entrance gate.

His anger was obvious. So was the fact Chloe hadn't been found. At his furious gesture, the other guards fanned out, clearly intending to search the city.

I pulled up fast, watching them go. I couldn't follow them; that would only get me 'escorted' back to my apartment in obedience to Ren's orders. And none of my friends in Nyciena would be any help. Their parents were too politically connected for them to want to risk their families' positions by offending the new king.

But if this was the Sylphaen...

I kicked hard in the water, taking off for the city wall.

They'd trapped me in a cave hundreds of miles north of here, but in that cave they'd had a setup intended for sacrificing her. Their crazy leader, Kirzan, had made their plan clear. And with a place like that, they probably wouldn't stay in the city long – especially since anyone with a brain could predict that Ren would have Nyciena searched the moment he learned Chloe was gone. So they'd go north. They'd sneak her out of the city somehow, and fast, and take her to their hideout to be killed.

Unless someone stopped them.

Houses and startled dehaians blurred as I twisted through the streets, and in only a few moments, the base of the veil came into view. Without more than a cursory glance to the sensors by the rocks to confirm that nothing human was around, I shot through the barrier.

At the edge of my senses, I could feel a single dehaian swimming toward the city. In the distance far above me, some fish drifted along in water that was nearly black from the night.

And otherwise, there was nothing.

Cursing, I raced north.

At best, they probably only had a few hours' head start. And depending on how they were bringing Chloe with them, transporting her might slow them down.

This would work.

I fought for more speed.

And felt the other dehaian turn to follow me.

Already racing, my heart found a way to go faster. Ren's soldiers hadn't stopped me through the entire length of town. They'd left me alone, either because they didn't want a fight or because they couldn't catch me.

One lone guard wasn't going to mess that up now.

"Zeke!"

I blinked.

"Dammit, Zeke, wait!"

I spun sharply, my momentum carrying me back through the water for several yards before I came to a stop.

Jirral swam toward me, breathing hard.

"I don't have time for this," I snapped. "Chloe's been–"

"Chloe's fine," he panted. "She... she's with me."

My brow drew down. "With you where?"

"At my camp. Outside the city." He swallowed hard. "Damn

you can swim, boy."

I ignored him. "What about the Sylphaen?"

He took another breath. "I shot the two holding her. The others escaped."

"Was one of them a gray-haired woman with blue scales?"

He hesitated. "One who got away, yes."

I swore. I really wanted to get my hands on Liana, though knowing she was dead would have been almost as good.

Because now she was still out there, where she could try to hurt my friends and family all over again.

"Where's this camp?"

"This way." He nodded toward the water behind him.

I started swimming in the direction he'd indicated. He hurried to keep up.

"What were you planning on doing if you had caught the Sylphaen?" Jirral asked.

Barely holding back a glare, I didn't respond.

"That was really stupid, Zeke. Racing off like that."

"What would you have preferred? Ren and his soldiers weren't going to help."

He paused. "You could have come looking for me."

My gaze flicked toward him before I could pull it back to the water in front of us. He didn't glance my way.

We swam on in silence. From the shadows, the hills started to emerge, their slopes barren of anything but the occasional pockmark of a cave.

"Up here," he said, swimming toward an opening high on

the side of a hill.

I spotted a glimmer of torchlight when we came close.

On a rough bed of seaweed, Chloe sat with her tail curled tight to her chest. Relief flashed across her face at the sight of us, followed swiftly by worry.

"Zeke." She pushed away from the bed, one hand clutching the torch and her smile wavering as though uncertain it should be there.

I hesitated, my eyes scanning over her. Purple shadows colored her torso and face where they shouldn't have, like the ghosts of bruises.

"Are you okay?" I demanded. "What happened? Did they hurt you?"

Her gaze went to Jirral for a heartbeat. "I'm fine."

I looked between them, hearing something in her voice that she wasn't saying.

"How are you?" she asked.

Annoyance hit me for the change of subject, and I gave a quick shrug. "Fine," I replied, though really, I probably wasn't. Everything had gone to hell in the past few hours. I didn't know what I was anymore.

She smiled again, with that same uncertain expression like she wasn't quite sure what to do. "And Niall and Ina?"

I didn't want to be talking about this. "Ina's fine too. Niall's still unconscious. His physician, Liana, she... well, I mean, she was the one who took you out of the pit, and we think maybe–"

"That was Niall's doctor?" she interrupted.

I nodded.

"But he's okay? She didn't try to–"

I shook my head. Chloe let out a breath, appearing relieved for a heartbeat before she looked back up at me.

"She was the one who poisoned your dad."

I could hear a question in the horrified statement. "I think so."

Chloe turned away.

I grimaced and then glanced to Jirral. "Did you see where Liana and–"

"Which way is it to Santa Lucina?"

I looked back at Chloe.

She was watching us both, her face intense.

"You can't–" I started.

"The Sylphaen killed your dad. They're after me. If I leave, maybe they'll–"

"Liana's been a palace physician for years," I protested. "There's nothing to say she did this because you were here."

"Except that she went to get me two seconds after your dad was dead."

"That still doesn't mean–"

"I don't want more people getting hurt, Zeke. You, Ina, your brothers…"

Her pained expression made me turn away. I didn't want anyone getting hurt either. Obviously. But that included her. It really did. The Sylphaen wouldn't stop, whether she was in

Nyciena or Santa Lucina, and if she was here, at least I could help.

And Santa Lucina wasn't remotely safe. They'd nearly killed her the last time she was there.

"But what about the neiphiandine?" I argued. "You can't go on land anyway and–"

"It might have worn off. And even if it hasn't, I'll just stay near the coast till it does."

"Alone?"

She blinked at me.

I grimaced, looking away again.

"They headed north," Jirral said into the silence. "But I don't know if they'll continue going that way."

Distractedly, I shook my head. "No, that's probably right. They have a cave up there."

"They may have other places to hide."

I hesitated. He could be right. Their leader, Kirzan, had chains and an altar and all sorts of psychotic junk up there for killing Chloe, but he could have more of the same elsewhere.

As comforting as *that* was.

I closed my eyes.

"I need to get back to land, Zeke," Chloe said quietly. "If I can get some distance from the ocean, the Sylphaen might have a harder time finding me. And your family... what if the Sylphaen *are* doing this because of me? Because I'm here?"

"Why kill the king just because you're in Nyciena?" I asked without looking at her.

She didn't respond.

"Because it's easier to do what you want in chaos than order," Jirral said.

I glanced to him.

"Assassins alter the status quo," he explained. "They disrupt things so another goal can be accomplished. Torvias had Chloe under guard, but as a guest of the palace despite Ren's assertion she was a spy. No one was going to challenge that, and finding a pretense for getting Chloe out of Nyciena..." He shrugged. "But with Torvias gone, suddenly there's confusion, a killer in our midst, and everyone becomes preoccupied. If you're Liana, you suddenly have the run of the place. You can do things you couldn't otherwise."

Jirral paused. "Chloe's right. She needs to get out of here."

I turned away from them both. This wasn't going the way I'd planned – though on measure, I didn't really know what I'd intended anyway.

Not this, though.

"My friends will help me get out of town," Chloe said. "I'll go as far from the ocean as I can stand and... and maybe the Sylphaen will leave you all alone."

She paused. "I'm sorry for this, Zeke. I am so, *so* sorry."

I looked up at her. "It's not your fault."

She gave me a grateful smile, though she didn't seem to believe me.

"It's the best option," Jirral said to me. "Given what she is, she can probably get farther inland than they'll be able to reach."

My brow furrowed. "Huh?"

Chloe looked down.

Jirral glanced between us, seeming surprised. "You didn't tell him?"

"I only found out yesterday," she explained defensively, as if repeating something she'd already said.

He paused. "Chloe is half-landwalker, Zeke."

I blinked.

"They're real," she told me. "My mom was one. The ocean makes them sick, so they keep away from it normally, but she... she didn't. I think that's why I could stay on land all those years, though. The dehaian stuff didn't start," she grimaced, as if searching for a word, "start waking up till I came to Santa Lucina."

I stared at her.

"Real-life legend," Jirral said. "Though from the stories, your friend shouldn't even be alive. Landwalkers aren't like humans; dehaians can have children with them, but the kids from those unions – *if* they even survive infancy – they never manage to change without dying."

The memory of what happened when she'd entered the water yesterday flashed through my mind, leaving me to wonder if that'd been the effect of the neiphiandine after all.

"Maybe that's why it hurt so much," she offered softly, as if reading my thoughts.

Jirral made a sympathetic noise. "There's a chance, though,

now that you've survived changing, that things might balance themselves back out for you. Let you remain on land longer than us, or go farther inland than we could reach. Possibly even stay in Kansas till the Sylphaen can be stopped."

"You think so?" Chloe asked, hope in her voice.

A breath escaped me.

He shrugged. "Maybe. Regardless, it'll be better if you put distance between you and Nyciena, before the Sylphaen try something else to get their hands on you."

Her hopeful expression melted into something almost pained at the words.

"It wasn't her fault," I snapped.

"No, of course not," Jirral agreed. "But she's still the reason they're–"

"I said it wasn't her fault."

The words were hard, and at them, he paused. I looked away, my heart pounding.

"It wasn't yours either, Zeke," he told me quietly.

I shook my head. I knew that. Ren had been an ass for suggesting otherwise.

Even if I had been the one to bring her here, knowing full well the Sylphaen were after her and that they'd do anything to get what they wanted.

I'd just believed Nyciena would be safe.

Drawing a breath, I pushed the thought away. Clearly, I'd been wrong. So wrong. She needed to get as far from here, from us, as possible. Back to that human boy, and her human friends, and everything there.

And who knew when she'd come back.

"Zeke..." Chloe tried.

"How far inland can you go?" I asked, the hard tone returning.

She hesitated, watching me, and then gave a small shrug. "I didn't feel too bad in Utah. Not like I did in Colorado, anyway."

I nodded. Hell of a lot farther than us, then.

"Good," I said. "Let's go."

"Now, hold on!" Jirral protested. "You can't leave this second!"

I ignored him and headed for the cave exit.

"Wait," Chloe said. I glanced back. "What about Ina and Niall? You need to be here for–"

"They have the guards," I replied. "And the Sylphaen... they're after you."

"But you–"

"I can take her back," Jirral said.

"No."

He studied me for a moment, and I could tell he knew what I was thinking. That it was good that he'd helped Chloe – helped her more than either of them were probably telling me – but he was still the last person I'd trust with anyone's safety.

His face darkened. "Zeke, this is foolish. You can't just go off on your own–"

"You good for travelling now?" I asked, turning back to Chloe.

"No, she's not," Jirral answered for her. "She needs to leave, yes, but not to race out of here this second."

Chloe glanced between us uncomfortably. "I-I'm okay, yeah."

Jirral made a frustrated sound. "You—"

"Fine," I said over top of him. "Then Jirral, you tell Ina to stay with Ren. Niall too, when he wakes up. And Chloe and I will—"

"You honestly think I'm just going to let you go out there on your own?" he interrupted.

"If you want to stop Ina or Niall from following me."

"You can't—"

"There aren't any guards to escort us, so don't try suggesting it. And my friends in Nyciena wouldn't dream of pissing Ren off by helping me. You're not exactly in the best shape for the speed we need to travel either, so—"

"Well, neither is she!" Jirral looked to Chloe. "You may think you're better. You may even feel better. But you're not. Sieranchine's effects are only as stable as the time you give them to sink in, and after what they did, that time is going to be a while. Push now, and you could tear muscles, rupture an organ, anything."

He turned to me. "Those Sylphaen beat her, Zeke. Blindfolded and cuffed her, beat her like hell, and then locked her in a box so they could take her away without anyone seeing. She could barely move when I found her, and that was an hour ago. So you tell me, is she good to travel now?"

I froze. Chloe looked away.

"I thought not," Jirral finished. "She's not going anywhere. Not until she's actually well. And neither are you."

He took the torch from Chloe roughly and headed over to wedge it into a crevice in the wall. "You go back to Nyciena, Zeke. To the palace and you stay there. Chloe and I will leave for Santa Lucina in a few days."

I was still watching Chloe. She wouldn't look at me.

"Zeke?"

I blinked, remembering to breathe, and I pulled my gaze to Jirral. "She's not going with you," I said, trying to regroup.

"Stop being a—"

"I said she's not!"

Shaking, I stared at him.

"You will stay," I continued to him, each word tight. "You will tell Ina not to leave the palace. Niall too. And I will go with Chloe once she's well enough to travel. Understand?"

He paused. "You are *so* like your father."

I didn't respond. I wasn't sure I could.

"I'll stay," he agreed. "On the condition that once he's well enough to move, I'm telling Niall where you went. And if he chooses to bring a hundred soldiers with him to guard your foolish ass and drag you back to Nyciena, so be it."

My teeth clenched. "Fine."

"Fine," he agreed. "Then I'll go make sure we're still safe

here."

He looked to Chloe. His gaze ran over her, as though he was deciding what to say, and then he just turned and swam out of the cave.

A breath left me. I glanced to her as she returned to the bed of seaweed. Sinking onto the leaves, she folded her tail in front of her like a human hugging their legs to their chest.

And she never once looked my way.

I shivered, my skin crawling at the idea of what they'd done to her. How they'd hurt her. I wanted to ask if she was okay, though I knew it was a stupid question. She'd been through hell since she'd found out she was dehaian.

No one would be okay.

I grimaced and turned back toward the cave entrance. None of this was her fault. My father's death, Ren's stupidity, or the fact that if I could have, I probably would've punched a hole through the cave wall right now.

It had nothing to do with Chloe.

She was just paying for it at every turn.

And if I ever got my hands on the Sylphaen who'd caused this…

With effort, I drew another breath. I'd get Chloe to safety. I'd do it, even if I still didn't like the idea of taking her to Santa Lucina. Then I'd get back here. I'd find Liana.

And this time I'd make sure she didn't escape.

12

CHLOE

My arms around my tail, I sat on the seaweed and tried not to feel uncomfortable with Zeke only a few yards away.

I failed.

His dad was dead. Without more help from a real doctor, Niall might soon be too. Zeke's world had gone to shambles in the space of a few hours.

And all because I was here.

I wanted to swim like crazy for Santa Lucina right this moment, if only to keep things from getting any worse.

But I remembered what Jirral had said.

My grip tightened on my tail. He had to be wrong, though. About the sieranchine, about all of it. I was fine. I may not know about their drugs, but I knew about me. And I was fine.

I wished he hadn't told Zeke what happened, though. I didn't want Zeke thinking he needed to worry about me. Not when everything else in his life was already a mess.

And anyway, I just really wanted to move on. Get back to

land and away from the dehaians, because the Sylphaen were hiding among them.

Could be any one of them.

I shivered. So I needed to leave. That was the important thing right now.

My insides quivered and I drew a breath, trying to keep the trembling at bay.

I'd get back to land, though. I'd get there and then everything would be fine.

My eyes closed, but that was just as bad. It made me feel like the hood was on my head again. Like someone might hit me again. Drawing a sharp breath, I opened my eyes, scanning the cave.

It really felt like the Sylphaen might come from the walls.

As irrational as that was.

I swallowed. I was fine. The sieranchine had worked, I was healed, and I was fine.

And now I needed to go.

"Zeke?"

By the cave entrance, he turned his head, though he didn't look at me.

I cleared my throat. "I wondered if maybe we could–"

"How many were there?"

I blinked. "How many…?"

"Sylphaen. The ones who hurt you."

On the seaweed, I shifted uncomfortably. It wasn't important. I didn't want to think about that.

"Chloe?"

"Zeke, I–"

He turned to me. A shiver ran through me at the look in his eyes.

Zeke meant to kill the Sylphaen the moment he found them. I could tell that as easily as if he'd said it aloud.

"How many?" he repeated.

"F-four."

"Was Liana one of those who hit you?"

I shook my head, not taking my eyes from him. "I don't think so."

He nodded and turned back to the cave entrance.

I waited, but he didn't speak again. "Look, um… I know what your grandfather said, but do you think maybe we could go ahead and–"

"We're not leaving yet."

I let out a breath. "I'm really fine. And maybe if we travel a bit slower than–"

He turned back toward me again, the answer clear on his face.

Frustration welled up in me, along with a trembling sort of rage that just made me want to scream.

Pushing away from the seaweed, I swam for the cave entrance.

Zeke rose quickly, blocking my path. "Chloe, you can't–"

I retreated, not wanting to be touched. My gaze darted around to find a way past him.

He tensed, watching me.

"I need to get back home, Zeke," I told him. "Please. I-I can't just stay here waiting for you, Ina, or Jirral to be the next person the Sylphaen—"

"Chloe."

Breathing hard, I met his sapphire eyes.

"They're not here because of you," he said gently. "I don't care what Jirral thinks. No one kills a king just because they want to get to one girl, no matter who that girl is. But if you go now…"

His gaze went to my cheek and his brow furrowed, as if he was searching for words.

I looked away.

"You need time too," he finished. "Please."

He motioned to the seaweed. I hesitated, and then sank to the ground near the cave entrance.

With a vaguely irritated sigh, he joined me.

"You'll feel it if someone comes near this place, right?" I asked after a moment.

He nodded.

"But the other side of the hill—"

"When Jirral gets back, he can keep an eye on that side."

I glanced to him. He sounded like he'd prefer if his grandfather stayed there.

"What… what is it between you two?" I asked hesitantly.

He looked away.

I winced. I shouldn't have asked. It was probably the wrong

thing to do. Almost certainly, in fact. But every time Zeke and Jirral were in the same room together, I felt like I was trapped in no-man's land while the two of them lobbed grenades at each other from the trenches.

And I really wanted to know why.

"Who was…" I tried to remember the name and failed. "That person he mentioned back at his house?"

"Miri."

Zeke's voice was quiet.

My discomfort grew. He sounded half-dead. "If you don't want to–" I started.

"She was my sister."

I shifted awkwardly.

"She died when I was seven."

He paused.

"We were visiting the Stovarlia Preserve. It's a place about half a day from here. Jirral had taken us to see the coral reefs. Me, Ina… and Miri. She was five."

He paused again, his gaze on the dark water beyond the cave.

"Driecaran spies found us. They'd bribed their way past the border. Learned of our plans. Their leaders were in a pretty vicious territory dispute with Dad and…" He exhaled. "And they thought this would give them leverage."

I shivered.

"They killed the guards with us so fast. I'd never seen anyone die before. And then they grabbed Miri. Jirral, though, he… he didn't fight them. He held onto me and Ina, and he just talked. Bargained. And did *nothing* as they took Miri away."

Zeke fell silent. I didn't move, uncomfortable at the idea of even making a sound.

"We don't do well out of water," he said finally. "People my age, older, we can survive maybe two or three weeks without any contact with the ocean. But much longer than that, and we grow weak. Our heart, lungs, all of it, they have trouble working anymore. It kind of looks like poisoning to humans. And for children, it… it happens faster. But the Driecarans wanted to pressure Dad, so they hid Miri on land and told him to concede to their demands or they'd let her die."

I stared at him. His voice was so distant.

"Dad refused. He told us that if he gave in to a small nation like Driecara, a nation that used spies more than soldiers to protect themselves, then more powerful territories would try what the Driecarans had done. Things were really tense in those days. None of the territories worked together; nothing was really safe. And Jirral's brother had just died, leaving Dad the throne since Jirral didn't want it, which meant all the other nations were angling to take advantage of the new king. So if he backed down…"

Zeke sighed. "Jirral, though… he kept urging Dad to negotiate. He insisted that we give the Driecarans what they wanted. Appeasement and all that. And when Dad wouldn't…" He shook his head. "Dad did everything he could, though. His soldiers found the ones who'd taken her, found out where she was, everything. The Driecarans had hidden her in a warehouse in Mexico, maybe fifteen miles from the shore. But for someone her age, someone so small…"

He shook his head. "She died before they got there."

My arms tightened around my tail.

"Dad went crazy. At least, that's what people say. The Driecarans had taken Miri because they had been sure he'd cave. They'd counted on it. And when he didn't, and Miri died… he made sure nothing like that would ever happen again."

"What did he do?" I whispered into the silence.

Zeke looked to me, his expression haunted by pain and old ghosts. "He wiped Driecara from the face of the Earth."

I swallowed as he turned back toward the ocean.

"The Driecarans should have been ready for it. Maybe they were and it didn't matter. But he called up all the soldiers we had and within the space of a year, everyone from the royal family to the lowest politician had been hunted down. The entire country was destroyed. And their people… their people fled. If they survived."

Zeke ran a hand through his black hair. "Jirral called him a genocidal maniac, and that was about the nicest thing. And my mom… she couldn't take what he did, couldn't take what happened to Miri or any of it, so she left. Went back to her family in Lycera. Everything kind of fell apart. And I know what Dad did was wrong. He was trying to keep us safe, but the way he accomplished that…"

I shivered.

"Jirral should have stopped them from taking Miri in the first place, though. Or… or at least just let them…"

I paused, almost certain I could hear the words he wasn't saying.

"Take you?" I asked carefully.

His head turned, though he didn't meet my gaze.

And I didn't know what to do. He had to know they would have killed him. Or that he probably couldn't have survived on land any better than his little sister. Not when he'd only been seven years old.

He had to know that.

It just didn't seem like he cared.

"I'm sorry," I said. "I shouldn't have brought it–"

"You have a right to know. Everyone else already does."

I wasn't sure how to respond.

Silence stretched between us.

"We just need to stay here a few days," he said quietly. "Let the sieranchine work. And then we'll leave. Okay?"

My brow furrowed. "And you're going to be here the whole time? What about Ina and Niall? Won't they worry?"

Zeke shifted uncomfortably, not meeting my gaze. "I can't go back. Not till this is over, anyway. Ren confined me to my apartment to keep me from looking for you, and if I head there now… it won't go well." He paused. "Just a few days, alright?"

I swallowed. "Okay."

He nodded, his eyes still on the ocean.

I looked down. I had to do what he wanted. After all that… I couldn't hope to argue without feeling like a monster.

Even if I'd wanted to.

They seemed totally carefree. Him, Ina and Niall. They seemed like they had everything anyone could want.

And they'd been through so much, I didn't even know where to begin.

My gaze slid to him. His black hair stirring in the current, he didn't take his eyes from the dark water outside.

I wanted to reach out to him. Maybe take his hand. Maybe just tell him it'd be alright. But I knew that was stupid. I'd practically just met him, despite all that we'd been through in the past day. And whatever everyone's opinion, at best he really was just a new friend. I couldn't invade his space like that.

And I couldn't promise anything would be alright.

My gaze fell to my lap and my fingers clasping each other there.

I'd wait a few days like he asked. But only that. And then we'd get back to Santa Lucina as fast as possible. Because everything else aside, he needed to be here. Even if Ren was angry at him, what was left of Zeke's family needed to be together right now.

And in the meantime I just had to hope that, before Zeke risked his life trying to kill any Sylphaen, the soldiers would reach them first.

13

ZEKE

In the end, Chloe gave it four days.

Barely.

Her bruises disappeared by the second morning, and she seemed to move more easily by the next evening. I caught her watching the cave entrance more often than not, though when she'd notice me studying her, she'd just blink and look away.

But she hardly slept.

Jirral tried encouraging her to rest. Told her it would help her body repair itself even if, as a dehaian, she'd normally only need to sleep every two or three days. But she wouldn't. Simply closing her eyes seemed to frighten her, and every time she did drift off, she'd jerk back awake again with her face as white as a sheet.

And she never let anyone touch her.

I'd noticed it a few days before, when she'd tried to bolt

out of the cave while Jirral was gone. Fear had flashed across her face as I'd come near, the expression so strong, it was like she thought I was a Sylphaen. She'd stayed away from both me and Jirral since he'd returned that first day, mostly remaining curled in the cave's corner while she waited for her body to heal.

It bothered me more and more as time went on. I didn't know why I let it, except that it was just another example of the damage the Sylphaen had done. Another way they'd hurt her.

One more thing they had to pay for.

"Stick to the southern line of Myriarch," Jirral said.

I blinked, pulling my attention back to him. By the cave entrance, Chloe hovered, waiting for Jirral to finish his instructions.

No matter how pointless they were.

"And don't try getting too close to the Riovarian hills. I spotted a few sharks that way last month and you don't want Chloe having to contend with them."

"We'll be fine," I told him tiredly, not bothering to add that I'd been to Santa Lucina a hundred times. Or that our spikes would tear through the hide of any shark stupid enough to attack, and that was if they were fast enough to catch us in the first place.

He knew all that.

"Huh," he commented. He swung his bag up from the floor and tossed it to me roughly. "Food, medicine and clothes, though the latter won't fit her, obviously. Try not to be such an idiot that she ends up needing to use all this stuff, eh?"

I took the bag and headed for the entrance.

"Thank you for your help, Jirral," I heard Chloe say as I passed.

She followed me out of the cave.

"How long will it take to get there?" she asked as the dark water swallowed the glow of the torchlight behind us.

"Most of a day."

"That's the fastest we could make it?"

I hesitated. There wasn't any way I was going to let us travel at top speed. "Safely, yes."

Her mouth tightened, but she didn't press it.

The hills and valleys surrounding Nyciena gradually fell behind us. I couldn't think what to say to her as the hours passed, and from her silence, she didn't seem to want to talk either. There wasn't much to discuss in any case. She'd leave the ocean, and anywhere near the coast, and stay away from both for as long as she could tolerate.

Which, given her history, might be years.

But that was what she needed to do to stay safe, and as a plan it obviously made the most sense, so there wasn't anything to talk about.

No matter how uncomfortable the idea made me.

We passed the flat terrain bordering the valleys of Myriarch and then turned to trace a long curve around the Riovarian hills, just in case. Everything Jirral said aside, Chloe didn't need the stress of learning how to take on a shark right now.

Though I honestly wouldn't have minded a good fight. I still felt like breaking something.

The water grew shallower as we rounded the outer perimeter of the hills. I could feel the temperature rising incrementally the farther we swam, though it was still sometime past midnight above the rolling waves.

Something moved to our right.

I glanced over sharply, and saw Chloe do the same.

"What–" she started.

I motioned her to silence, my attention on the hills.

A shape flicked between the slopes, too fast to be a shark.

I gestured to the seafloor, and then followed her when she dove toward the rocks below.

We dropped down behind a large boulder. Chloe's brow rose questioningly. Reaching into the bag, I didn't respond, instead drawing out the veil control stone and circling us with it quickly.

The veil swelled up, coming to a close over our heads.

A moment passed.

Three dehaians left the hills, swimming toward the place where we'd been. At my side, Chloe's breath caught.

They were Vetorians. Knife straps crossed their chests over top of so many scars, the old wounds and tribal markings looked like strange maps. The trio fanned out in the water, their heads turning while they scanned the area. Scales of sickly white and faded bronze covered their tails, and metal glinted from their fins, revealing the razor-sharp blades clipped there.

I glanced to Chloe. Her eyes were locked on them, and I could see her trembling.

My grip on the veil stone tightening, I stopped myself from reaching out to calm her. The veils deadened most noise, but I still didn't want to startle her into making a sound.

The mercenaries passed overhead without seeing us and continued on. My gaze returned to the hills.

Nothing moved.

I remained where I was. If the Vetorians had come out here because they'd spotted us earlier, the lack of motion now could just be a trap.

Chloe looked to me, her pale skin bloodless. I put a finger to my lips. She nodded.

Seconds turned to minutes.

The Vetorians emerged from the murky twilight to our left, swimming back toward the hills. A string of fish trailed behind them.

I drew a slow breath when they disappeared behind the hillsides. I let another minute pass for good measure, watching both the hills and the ocean around us alike, but nothing changed. With a glance to Chloe, I motioned for her to stay low, and at her nod, I switched off the veil surrounding us.

We emerged from the shelter of the boulder and took off.

Water rushed around us as we raced along the seafloor. I kept an eye to Chloe, watching for any sign that the speed hurt her, and when miles separated us and the hills, I finally motioned for us to stop again.

"You okay?" I asked.

She nodded, though she was breathing hard and still looked pale. "More mercenaries?"

I didn't know what to say. They shouldn't have been here, just like they shouldn't have come near us on the way home a few days ago. I knew Ren said they'd been breaking past the borders, but for them to be *this* far inside Yvaria…

"Zeke?"

"We're fine," I answered, hoping I was right.

Worry tightened her face. "So this is normal?"

I hesitated, searching for an explanation to make us both feel better. "No," I admitted. "But they're probably just stragglers hiding out after getting past the border patrol. The soldiers will catch them soon."

Chloe didn't respond. Not knowing what else to do – and not really wanting to talk about it anyway – I started swimming again.

She followed.

It wasn't like Vetorians hadn't gotten past the borders before. It was rare, but it'd happened over the years. But for them to be here in *these* numbers, and swimming around so damn-near brazenly…

It almost felt like someone was letting them in.

I swallowed, pushing the thought away. Liana and her three cohorts aside, the whole world wasn't in a conspiracy.

Especially not one of that scale.

So this was an anomaly. A disturbing one, but one that – like everything else – I'd deal with when I got home.

When Chloe was gone.

A grimace twisted my face and it took effort to drive it away. She had to go back. It was the safest option left.

Trying to make myself believe the words, I continued toward Santa Lucina.

14

CHLOE

My sides ached from the hours of swimming, but I wasn't about to tell Zeke. Anyone's muscles would be tired after how long we'd been traveling, which meant it probably had nothing to do with old injuries or the sieranchine. So I wasn't going to mention it.

Because according to what he'd told me a few miles before, Santa Lucina was only minutes away.

I didn't know what I'd say to Noah when I saw him again. Or Baylie, either – assuming she hadn't headed back to Reidsburg already. Noah, at least, knew what I was. For Baylie, the fact I'd disappeared for days on end would require some hefty explanation, even if I did tell her the truth.

And I wasn't sure about that. I didn't want to lie to her, but I still couldn't figure out how to tell someone I'd known my whole life that, oh, by the way, I happen to be a mermaid.

I didn't want to have that conversation. After days of being surrounded by dehaians, I'd started to feel fairly normal in my new form, but once I was back on land and back in Reidsburg where everyone was human, all that would go away. I'd be a freak again.

A freak who couldn't be away from the ocean for long without a crazy-making compulsion to return to the water.

There wasn't any choice, though. The Sylphaen were here. I needed to get away from them.

Even if it meant I'd end up as the only dehaian in over a thousand miles.

My brow furrowed. I couldn't help that. People had been killed because I was here. So I'd just have to figure it out. Make living away from the sea work for however long it took for the Sylphaen to be stopped. My parents had been nuts about the water, mostly because they thought I'd die if my dehaian side woke, but surely they'd loosen up now that I'd survived changing. Maybe they'd even help me.

And in the meantime, I'd get to see Noah again.

My gaze flicked to Zeke. A pang of discomfort hit me as I tugged my gaze away again.

I wanted to leave. There wasn't anything to debate.

"So," I called. "When do we see if the neiphiandine is gone?"

Zeke blinked, as though I was pulling him from his thoughts. "What?"

"The neiphiandine. When should we check if it's gone?"

He hesitated. "Now's good, I guess. There's still a few minutes till we're in sight of the coast."

"Okay."

I swam upward. A heartbeat passed before he followed.

Pale sunrise lit the waves as we came to a stop several yards below the surface, and the current pulled at us, gradually urging us toward the distant shore. I blinked at the glare of the light, my eyes stinging.

"Okay," Zeke said, watching the water above us. "Just take it slow, eh?"

"What do I do?"

"Well, *if* the neiphiandine has worn off at all, you should be able to change your lungs and skin enough to handle the air up there. But you shouldn't need to think about it too much. Your body will know what to do."

My eyebrow inched up worriedly, but he just swam for the surface. I hesitated, and then followed.

The water rolled above my head, dipping toward me and then rising again as the waves swept along. Several feet higher, Zeke glanced around in the open air, and then motioned for me to come up beside him.

I drew a breath and kicked upward.

My head broke the surface.

Air scorched my skin. The nascent sunrise burned my eyes. I couldn't breathe.

Gasping, I fell back beneath the waves.

Zeke dove down and caught me.

"No," I protested, pushing his hands aside. "No, I'm going to do it."

"The drugs haven't–"

I shot back upward.

"Chloe!"

Air clogged my lungs, thicker than anything the blindfolds had created. Pain scraped along my skin like a sunburn under sandpaper. I choked, squeezing my eyes shut as I fought to stay above the waves.

My fingers curled into fists as the burning increased. I would change like I needed to. I'd swim back to Santa Lucina and get away from the ocean. I was not going to let this damn drug interfere with what had to happen.

The pain lessened.

I gasped and then coughed at the dense air.

Which grew thinner with every heartbeat.

I opened my eyes. The light glared and then weakened, becoming the ordinary pale glow of sunrise.

A thrilled cry escaped me. I'd done it. I'd beaten the neiphiandine.

"Are you alright?" Zeke asked from a few feet away.

I nodded. "Yeah, I think... I think it's gone. I–"

A sizzle of pain scraped over my skin and I winced. Breathing hard, I closed my eyes, ordering my skin not to change back again.

"Don't push too hard," he warned.

I shook my head, not wanting to hear it. I was going to beat this.

My breathing slowed as the pain faded again. I opened my

eyes to find him watching me, worry on his face.

"Chloe, maybe you shouldn't–"

"Ready to keep going?"

Zeke hesitated. "Yeah," he answered tightly.

He dove back down.

I stayed where I was for a moment, gulping in air thicker than normal but more breathable than it'd been in days. The wind brushed my skin, its passage still stinging a bit, while in the distance, sunrise brightened the horizon.

A smile tugged at my lips. I sank beneath the water and took off after Zeke.

He didn't say anything when I pulled alongside him.

"Thanks for your help," I said after a moment passed.

He nodded.

We continued on. My heart began pounding harder as the water became shallower and the seafloor crept toward us.

"How much farther?" I asked into the silence.

"Almost there."

Another moment slid by.

"Are we heading for the house?"

"See for yourself," he offered with a wry look to the surface.

I hesitated at his tone, and then swam up.

We were only about a mile away.

The sun glowed behind the mountains on the horizon. Deep red and gold lit the undersides of the clouds, while the sky brightened to paler gradients of blue with every heartbeat.

The beach was cast with shadows from the homes and palm trees around it, and only a few early morning tourists speckled the sand.

But Noah's house was straight ahead.

I dove back down and pulled up beside Zeke again.

He glanced to me and kept swimming.

"What do you want to do if your friends aren't home?" he asked neutrally.

"Find somebody with a cell phone and call them, I guess."

He didn't respond.

From the corner of my eye, I studied him. I hadn't listened to him earlier about the neiphiandine, but surely he could see how I'd needed to do that? To try to get over that drug before we reached land?

"Is something wrong?" I asked.

He hesitated just a bit too long. "No."

For another moment, I watched him. "Okay."

"Ready?" he asked in the same weird tone.

I nodded.

We swam toward the shore.

∽ 15 ∾

NOAH

The sky lightened as the sun crept toward the mountaintops behind me, though deep shadows still engulfed the yard. Seagulls cried overhead, their calls the only other sound besides the waves rushing into shore.

On the edge of the bluffs, I didn't move. Exhaustion weighed on me. I'd been up half the night, just like most of the other nights before this. In all of their crafting, the old bastards who'd made my kind hadn't managed to give us the dehaians' ability to go without sleep, and I was really starting to feel it.

But there was nothing to be done. My cousins may have been dumb as rocks, and between all four of them they only made one brain, but that didn't mean they couldn't keep watch in shifts for days on end.

I drew a breath, blinking tiredly in the early morning light. It'd been over five days since Chloe left, and every one of them had been stressful. The moment Chloe's parents had been cleared by the doctors, they'd fled to Kansas to recover, and hopefully they were doing better than they had been. Baylie had stayed for a night at the hospital, under observation after her run-in with the dehaians and their chloroform. It'd taken a fair bit of convincing for Diane to get her to come back to our house, and I still wasn't sure it'd been the right decision. Dad thought we needed to talk to her, though, before she went home and told her own father what her stepbrothers really were.

Which might have been a good idea, except for the part where she wouldn't speak to me or Maddox at all.

And Chloe was missing.

At least, that's what we'd told the cops after they arrived at the cabin. We said she'd been kidnapped; taken just before Maddox and I had reached the ambulance. We'd claimed Chloe must have stabbed one of them somehow – the closest thing to the truth in our entire story – but that another kidnapper had run off with her after the crash. I'd supposedly rushed away in the car to catch up with the unseen abductors, though of course I'd ultimately failed. Amber Alerts and manhunts were underway now, and the police told us they were doing everything possible to find her.

I really hoped they'd give up soon. They were needed on actual cases, and I hated that we'd had to lie.

Sunlight spread over the water, turning it to rippling gold. In the house behind me, I could feel the cousins moving around, changing shifts yet again.

I stifled a yawn. Maddox would be coming in a few minutes. He'd keep an eye out for her through the rest of the morning, just as he had for all the others since she'd left. He'd hardly said a word about the fact she was dehaian, and didn't seem to care any more than I did about our grandfather's stories. Our cousins' presence grated on him too, and he seemed perfectly happy to make certain they couldn't get their hands on Chloe.

While I'd just started to hope she didn't come back.

My stomach twisted. I wanted to see her again. I wanted more than that by far. And I didn't want to do what my dad had demanded: make sure she never returned here again. But new fears had crept up in the past few days of endless watching in case she arrived. Dad seemed to have no intention of sending my cousins packing anytime soon, and if there was even one minute when Maddox or I weren't around and those guys saw her first...

They'd tear her apart. They'd fight over her like a pack of hungry wolves. I'd seen them when we were kids, torturing animals they found near their cabin on the Washington coast. Seeing how much pain the creatures could take, at least until my dad came around. Then it was all just accidents and trying to help the poor, brutalized things. A mixture of their father and luck had kept them from expanding their interest to humans over the years, but Richard wouldn't do a thing about a dehaian.

Not when I suspected he had nearly as wide a sadistic

streak as his sons.

So Chloe had to leave. There wasn't a choice. My father had let the bastards stay, and now nothing here was safe.

I just hoped I'd have time to explain before she needed to go.

Scales and a fin flashed in the sunlight.

I tensed, my heart clenching while my vision sharpened on the spot a mile from shore. A moment passed while the water rippled and rolled, and nothing else appeared to differentiate those waves from any others.

But that'd been a dehaian. I was sure of it. More than that, it was her. I didn't know why, but I was certain it was her.

And my cousins thought so too.

I could feel them in the guest room, racing for the bedroom door. They'd be downstairs any second, and at the speed I'd heard dehaians could swim, I knew she'd be here soon too.

And then they'd catch her.

They'd finally get a dehaian to kill.

I shoved up from the ground and ran for the stairs.

∽ 16 ∾

CHLOE

I knew we had to be getting close to the shore. The seafloor was rising toward us steadily as we swam, and through the waves overhead, the sky was easy to see.

And after so long of intending to come back, I couldn't keep my heart from racing at the fact we were almost there.

Zeke finally slowed, and so I did as well. His scales and tail vanished as though washed away by the water, becoming swim trunks and legs.

He glanced to me.

I looked back at my tail, willing it to disappear like his had done.

Nothing changed.

Gritting my teeth, I glared at the cream scales that refused to leave.

"Chloe…"

"I can do this."

Treading water beneath the waves, he looked away.

I drew a sharp breath, returning my focus to my body, imagining my legs coming back and the scales taking the form of a swimsuit like Ina had told me they could.

A shiver ran through me.

The scales melted away. Instinctively, my muscles obeyed new commands as my tail split and my fin vanished into legs and feet. My skin reappeared, interrupted only where cream-toned scales still covered me like a shimmering swimsuit.

I tensed, suddenly frightened I wouldn't be able to breathe under the water anymore.

"You're still okay," Zeke assured me. "Just relax."

I looked over to him, and carefully pulled in a tiny breath.

It felt like every other one for the past day.

"Changing is like a spectrum," Zeke explained. "Lots of levels between human and full dehaian form."

Taking in deeper breaths, I didn't respond.

"Come on," he said, that tight tone returning to his voice.

We kept swimming. The seafloor came close enough to touch. My feet sank into the sand and I straightened, rising from the water.

Noah was running toward us across the beach.

A smile broke out across my face and I pushed past the tide to reach him. Atop the bluff, a house door slammed.

He caught my arms as I came close.

And he shoved me back toward the water.

I stumbled and fell into the surf.

"Hey!" Zeke protested, coming toward us.

Noah ignored him. "Get away. Get out of here now."

I pushed to my feet as he threw a look over his shoulder. "Noah, what—"

"Go, dammit!" he cried as he turned back to me. His eyes met mine, pain-filled disgust twisting his face. "Get the hell away from me, you scaly, scum-sucking fish. Don't you ever come near here again."

I froze, speechless.

"I said go!" he yelled, running at me.

Zeke rushed between us. "Back off, asshole!"

Red light flared in Noah's eyes and fiery cracks raced through his skin. With a snarl, he hurled Zeke back, sending him crashing into the waves thirty feet away.

"Go or die," Noah growled at me.

Breathless, I stared at him.

And then I spun and dove back into the water.

The ocean enveloped me and the change sizzled through my body. My tail kicked hard, throwing sea foam back at him and propelling me beneath the rolling tide.

Zeke raced up to me, spikes on his arms and fury in his eyes. "Are you alright?"

I drew a sharp breath, fighting back tears. I shook my head, not sure what to say.

He took my arm. "Come on," he said with a dark glance to the shore.

I nodded. With Zeke still holding onto me, I fled back out to sea.

17

NOAH

The cracks faded from my skin as Chloe vanished into the waves.

Something slammed into me from behind.

Water filled my mouth, followed by sand as I crashed down. A fist like a rock hammered down on my back, and then another sent an explosion of light across my vision when it pounded into my head.

Heat raced through my body. Pain retreated to nothing and adrenaline flooded my veins as every muscle tensed with the overwhelming desire to kill whatever was attacking me.

I never felt so alive as when I let my greliaran side free.

Snarling, I shoved away from the ground and something tumbled from my back. I spun, my heightened vision zeroing in on the nearest thing that had threatened me. The nearest thing I could tear to shreds.

Brock, the youngest of my cousins and the only one close to me in age, scrambled to his feet several yards away. Cracks

181

showed in his skin, with smoke and light pouring from them. Beneath his dark, buzz cut hair, his eyes were red-hot coals. On the beach, his older brothers watched us, unchanged yet, but with rage clear on their faces.

A growl slipped from me.

"You *bastard*," Brock spat, the words barely human through his gritted teeth. "That scaly bitch was ours and–"

I slammed into his chest, driving him to the ground, and my fists followed. Blood swirled in the tide rushing past.

One of his brothers grabbed me, hurling me aside. I hit the sand and rolled to my feet.

Wyatt stood beside Brock, who was climbing from the waves with blood dripping from the corner of his mouth despite his defenses. By the bluffs, the middle brothers, Owen and Clay, both watched me.

"Well, come on," Wyatt taunted. "You little dehaian fucking–"

I ran at him.

Owen crashed into my side. I tumbled into the water and then scrambled back up, lunging at him. His hands caught me, and his feet skidded through the sand with the effort of stopping my momentum. Twisting in his grasp, I tried to knock him off balance, but he wouldn't give.

Wyatt slammed into me, throwing me back to the ground again, and then Clay was there. White light burst across my vision as he drove his fist into my face.

And then he disappeared.

I shoved to my feet.

Maddox stood between us, his hands raised to keep us apart. By his brothers, Clay was pushing away from the ground.

"Back off," Maddox snapped.

Contempt curled Wyatt's mouth.

Fissures spread through Maddox's skin. "I said, back off."

"And what're you going to do if we don't?" Wyatt sneered.

The fissures grew. "You don't want to find out," Maddox replied quietly.

Wyatt paused, looking Maddox up and down. He gave a disgusted scoff. "You're not worth it." His gaze slid to me. "And you... well. Your precious dehaian bitch came back. Who knows? Maybe she will again." He smiled. "This isn't over. And we're not going anywhere."

With a jerk of his chin toward his younger brothers, he turned and headed for the stairs.

Barely restraining a growl, I watched them walk away, my muscles shaking with the desire to go after them and end the problem once and for all.

"Noah."

I twitched, Maddox's voice like an annoying buzz in my ear.

"Breathe, dammit," he ordered in a low tone. "Get a hold of yourself. Someone might see."

The growl escaped.

"Noah!"

I drew a sharp breath. I closed my eyes, struggling to do as he said.

The heat faded. The vivid rush of sensation from the world around me did as well. I trembled as my skin returned to normal and when I opened my eyes, the colors were dull enough for me to be sure my greliaran side was gone.

I winced, the pain of that first punch returning.

"What happened?" Maddox asked.

Lifting a hand to rub my jaw, I didn't respond.

"Wyatt said Chloe was here?"

He waited.

"Noah?"

I nodded. "Her and some dehaian guy, yeah."

"Will she be back?"

"I doubt it."

Maddox paused. I glanced over at him, and his mouth tightened as he read between the very short lines.

He sighed. "I'm sorry."

I nodded again, not wanting to talk about it. I hated what I'd said to her. What I'd done. But there hadn't been time, and if she'd stayed even a second longer...

Nausea twisted my stomach. My cousins had tried to take their frustration out on me, but it wasn't anything compared to what they would have done if they'd gotten their hands on her.

But that look on her face. Confused. Hurt.

Terrified.

I couldn't stop seeing it.

"Come on," Maddox said quietly.

I shook my head, my gaze going back to the ocean. "I'll be inside in a minute."

He hesitated and then nodded. Clasping a hand to my shoulder briefly, he turned and walked to the stairs.

I closed my eyes, an ache pressing down on me that had nothing to do with my cousins' fists. She wouldn't be back. Not after what I'd said or the way she'd looked at me. And maybe that would keep her safe. From my kind, anyway.

It was all I could do for her.

Even if it meant she hated me.

18

CHLOE

We swam on, and I barely saw the seafloor change beneath us as it went from empty sand to outcroppings of rock.

I couldn't understand it. Noah. Why he'd just...

"This way," Zeke said quietly.

He turned, leading me toward a mound of boulders jumbled together in a precarious mess. Dipping low in the water, he slid through a dark opening at the base of the pile. I followed.

The rocks closed in around me, and then opened into a cave. In the darkness, I felt Zeke swim to one corner, shrugging the bag from his shoulder as he moved. He retrieved something from inside, and then let the bag sink to the floor.

Blue-white light flooded the space, making rainbows sparkle from the fissures of ore in the stones around us. Reaching up, Zeke notched the torch into a crack in the cave wall.

I sank down, sitting on a small shelf of rock. My gaze wandered across the light playing over my scales.

"Are you okay?" he asked.

I didn't respond. I still wasn't sure what to say.

"Fucking asshole," Zeke muttered.

I opened my mouth and then caught myself, not wanting to sound like a girl defending her jerk boyfriend. Especially when, truth was, I didn't even know what to call him. Boyfriend. A guy I'd kissed. Something else that didn't have a category.

Psycho who'd been so kind a few days ago and now inexplicably hated the sight of me.

"What the hell was he, anyway?" Zeke continued.

"Greliaran," I answered without looking up.

"Which is?"

I gave a helpless shrug. "That."

Silence fell between us. My grip tightened around the edge of the rough stone shelf.

I didn't get it. How could someone change so completely? There had to be a reason. Something I wasn't seeing. Something that could have prompted him to just—

Cold horror spread through me and set my heart racing.

I looked to Zeke.

"What?" he asked, alarmed at my expression.

"Ina. She said we... we have this thing. Magic thing. Ava... ave-something. She said it feels all great for dehaians, but for humans it's like a drug. Makes them fall for us. Like, if we just want them to." I gulped down a breath. "So, what if I did that to him? Accidentally, I mean. What if I made him like me, and then he woke up from it and–"

Zeke swam over, catching my hands. "No, no, aveluria doesn't work like that."

I stared at him.

"It doesn't," he repeated. "Trust me."

"How do you know? You've done it?"

He hesitated. "Once. But not much. And that's not my point. People don't come out of it like that. They're either confused and not sure what happened, or they… you know…"

"Die."

He nodded uncomfortably.

"Did the person you used it on die?"

"Chloe, I – no, she didn't. She was fine. But I'm trying to tell you, that's not what happened here. You didn't cause this."

"Why would you do that to someone?"

Zeke paused. "Because I was trying to get past security to save a friend's life."

I looked down. Of course it was something like that. Zeke had never given me any reason to think he would hurt somebody that way.

But then, Noah had seemed like a good person too, until about twenty minutes ago.

Tears stung. I closed my eyes.

"You didn't do anything to deserve the way he treated you, Chloe," Zeke told me quietly.

I didn't respond.

"Hey." He put a hand to my cheek. "You didn't."

I looked up, meeting his insistent gaze. I managed a small nod.

He nodded as well, and for a moment, his eyes studied my face. His brow flickered down, and then he drew a short breath. Taking his hand away, he swam back to where he'd left the bag by the far wall.

"We should be safe here till you decide where to go next," he said, his voice tight.

I turned away, not wanting to think about it.

"So I... I'll just go find us some food," he continued, drawing a rope and some stone hooks from the bag. "Jirral's provisions aren't that great and there's usually–"

"Zeke?" I called, nervousness gripping me as he headed for the opening to the cave. I didn't want to be here by myself in the middle of nowhere.

I didn't want him to leave as well.

He glanced back.

"Don't?"

He hesitated, and then set down the rope. He swam toward me, pausing at the stone ledge for a heartbeat as though he didn't know what to do, and then he sank down by my side.

A moment crept past.

"Bad few days, eh?" I tried.

A small scoff escaped him as he watched the blue flames. "Yeah."

And I didn't know what else to say.

Shadows and torchlight danced on the sand of the floor.

Beyond the cave entrance, the current rushed over the rocks with a whispering sound.

I closed my eyes. A shudder ran through me, making my breath catch, while something so much heavier than exhaustion pressed down on my body like a blanket of lead. I knew I needed to keep moving. Get to land as fast as I could. The safety of anyone near me pretty much depended on it.

But I was tired. So tired. I hadn't slept in days and everything in the world was painful right now. I didn't know where to go anymore, or what I wanted at all, except maybe for the fresh hells of people hurting me every time I turned around to finally end.

Tears leaked from beneath my eyelids to join the saltwater.

"Hey," Zeke said quietly, taking my hand.

I looked over.

"Please don't cry," he urged. "It's going to be alright, I promise."

I gave a tiny nod, wanting desperately to believe him despite everything that'd happened so far.

He echoed the motion, his eyes not leaving mine.

A moment passed. He didn't look away. His brow twitched down, as though he was struggling with something, and he swallowed hard as he began to draw his hand back.

My fingers tightened on his. I didn't want him to go. It felt good to have him here. Comforting. Safe.

And more than that...

He paused. Questions flickered through his eyes. His other

hand lifted to my cheek again. He drew closer to me even as I moved toward him.

Gently, his lips met mine.

Warmth spread through me. A quiver tightened my stomach and chest, the sensation fluttery and amazing and desperate to grow. And I wanted it. More of it. My hand reached up, finding his side, holding him for fear he'd pull away and make this disappear.

His mouth pressed harder to mine as his fingers moved through my hair, gripping me as though he never wanted to let go. My body turned, leaving the ledge and meeting him as he rose as well. His hands slid around my back, pulling me to his smooth chest, and his tail pressed against me, contouring to every curve. My skin tingled with pleasure everywhere he touched it, the feeling building in intensity till it was all I could do to breathe.

I didn't know what I was doing.

The thought wasn't welcome. I didn't care. I wanted him touching me. Holding me.

This wasn't right.

I gasped, my mouth breaking from his. "I-I'm sorry. I..."

He drew back and let me go, the confusion on his face swiftly transforming into regret.

I turned away. It was too hard to look at him. I wanted his hands on me again. The desire for it was agonizing.

"I'm sorry," I repeated.

"Chloe..."

I felt the water move as he came up behind me. His fingers neared my shoulder and I flinched away.

A breath left him.

I looked back.

The pain in his eyes was worse than anything.

"Me too," he said quietly.

Turning, he swam from the cave.

A choked sob escaped me. Tears stung my eyes.

I sank to the ground and cried.

19

ZEKE

For a hundred yards, I swam, before anger and frustration kept me from going any farther.

I couldn't believe I'd been such an idiot.

Such a *complete* idiot.

Spinning to a stop, I hovered in the water, shaking.

I shouldn't have done that. Kissed her. Let myself and the aveluria and everything else just go like that. I should have been smarter. She was hurting. This wasn't the time.

What the hell had I been *thinking?*

My fist swung back, hitting the boulder behind me. I *hadn't* been thinking. That was the answer. I'd let the sight of her pain and the need to take it away drive me when I should have been using my brain.

And instead, I'd made it worse. Like an idiot, I'd just made it all worse.

My fist struck the stone harder. I couldn't believe myself. She didn't need this from me right now.

But when I'd touched her... when she'd moved toward me...

I grimaced, trying to push the memory away. Because it didn't matter. Her touch. Her taste. The warmth of her against me when every inch of her incredible body had pressed to mine...

Cursing, I kicked away from the seafloor. I was never going to be able to come near her *again* at this rate.

Breathing hard, I scanned the ocean around me. I needed something, *anything*, to get my mind off this.

Three shapes paused in the water at the edge of my senses.

And then they turned, heading my way.

My blood went cold and I swore, damning the universe's sick sense of humor. Vetorians had *not* been the kind of distraction I'd meant.

Of course, it could be Ren's soldiers this time.

Like it mattered.

Twisting in the water, I dove and pulled up just shy of the seafloor. Kicking up as little dust as I could, I flicked my tail and took off, weaving through the boulders.

I really hoped Chloe hadn't left the cave.

Torchlight flickered in the entrance. I darted through the opening.

Chloe looked up, hurt and alarm on her face in equal measure.

"Company," I told her as I swam across the cave. "Coming this way."

Her breath caught. She pushed away from the ground.

Snagging the torch from the wall, I jammed it quickly into the sand, extinguishing the blue flames. The cave plunged into darkness.

I turned. Chloe hovered in the center of the cave, watching me with her body silhouetted by the paler water beyond the entrance and her green eyes glowing ever-so-faintly in the darkness. Swiftly, I swam back and took her arm, drawing her with me. "Stay behind me," I whispered.

She didn't argue.

I inched my head from the cave opening, straining to feel any motion nearby.

Something shot through the water and I jerked back.

A pod of tentacle-ropes burst against the stone behind where I had been.

Chloe gasped. Outside, I heard a distant click, and then the sound of someone swearing in a Prijoran Zone dialect when nothing happened.

"Go!" I ordered.

Shouting broke out behind us as we sped from the cave and took off, twisting between the boulders scattered across the ocean floor. Pods flew through the water at our backs and splattered on the rocks in masses of brown webbing.

I could feel the Vetorians coming.

And merciful waves, were they fast.

My grip on Chloe tightened as I fought for more speed. Several hundred yards ahead, the open water waited, devoid of cover for miles. I could hear her gasping beside me, straining to keep up as I swam.

But the mercenaries were gaining.

"Keep going!" I yelled, shoving her ahead of me.

Carried by momentum, she floundered and then spun to look back in alarm.

"Do it!" I shouted over the distance between us. "Go!"

Spikes grew from my arms. I turned to see the mercenaries charging through the water like torpedoes from hell.

"Zeke!" Chloe yelled.

I looked back.

"Go, Chloe," I told her.

And then I raced at the Vetorians.

～ 20 ～

CHLOE

The three mercenaries sped through the water.

And Zeke swam right for them.

Like a snake, he cut sharply to the side as he came close and then swung out, striking at the nearest one. But the man just rolled, avoiding his spikes and then lashing out at Zeke with his knife-edged fin. Twisting away, Zeke darted around and sliced at him again.

His spikes caught the man's tail. Blood clouded the water.

The dehaian shouted with pain, and one of his companions spun back. But the other kept on, coming straight at me.

Knives glinted in his fists.

The other two circled Zeke, drawing their own knives as they moved. Feinting toward him, they slashed out, testing his speed, waiting for an opening.

And there was no way he would escape them both.

A breath left my chest. Through my body, a stillness spread.

The Vetorian rushed at me and I dove, my tail scraping his

as I narrowly avoided his grasp. Pain flickered at the edge of adrenaline as the blades on his fin grazed my scales, but I kept moving. He gave an angry cry as I sped off, and I could feel him spin in the water, trying to chase me down.

Spikes tingled from my arms. I charged at the other dehaians.

Their attention was on Zeke. Their knives were pointed at him. The man behind me yelled a warning.

But then it was too late.

My spikes slashed deep into the back of the mercenary Zeke had wounded, and the man howled. His companion's eyes went wide as the guy floundered and went still. Regrouping fast, the surviving mercenary flinched toward me as I curved in the water toward him.

Zeke didn't wait. He darted to the other side, his arm swinging with deadly precision.

A cry escaped the mercenary, the sound strangling itself as pain took over. I twisted around while Zeke swam up beside me fast, his gaze on the third guy.

The man kicked backward, coming to a stop in the water. His eyes went from me to Zeke, something almost like fear past the rage on his face.

And then he spun and raced away.

Breathing hard, I looked back, but the other two were gone, sinking toward the seafloor.

And their bodies were collapsing.

I stared in horror. Like hollow shells with the air sucked

out, their skin and bones pulled in on themselves, drying up and crumpling the bodies till nothing dehaian or human in appearance remained. As they hit the seafloor, the decay continued, compressing them even as they merged with the grit and sand.

"We're magic," Zeke explained quietly. "We have it in our bodies, our bones. It keeps the pressure out, enables us to survive outside the veils, but when we die and it fades..."

I swallowed. Nausea tried to argue, determined to rise back up my throat, and it took everything I had to keep it down.

He looked over at me. "Thank you."

I hesitated. I wasn't sure how to respond. He could have been killed. What else could I have done? Even now, there was a slice on his chest where a mercenary's knife had grazed him, and it hurt to see it. "You too," I answered.

He gave a small shrug, seeming calm if not for the fact his skin was abnormally pale.

Silence fell between us, heavy and awkward.

"I'm sorry, though," he continued uncomfortably. "You know, about..."

His hand twitched toward my arm.

I looked down. A trace of blood still clung to my spikes.

Shivers raced through me, whether from revulsion or fading adrenaline, I didn't know. I'd just wanted to stop them. To keep them from using their knives on Zeke.

And I'd killed someone.

Again.

The trembling grew stronger.

From the corner of my eye, I saw Zeke reach for me and then catch himself. Regret on his face, he drew his hand away.

"It's not the first time," I whispered.

His brow furrowed.

"The Sylphaen who injected me. I… I killed the first one who tried. I didn't mean to. He just… we were in an ambulance and he grabbed me. He was choking me. Trying to stick the needle in my neck. I was so scared." A shaky breath left me. "And the spikes came out."

Zeke was quiet for a moment. "They want you dead."

I glanced over at him.

"You're their sacrifice," he said. "Their goal is for you to die." He gave another small shrug. "Instead, you stayed alive."

I didn't know what to say.

His gaze dropped to the bodies now lost in the sand of the seafloor. "We should go. Get the bag and get out of here before that other one brings back friends."

I nodded. We swam back between the boulders, and when we reached the cave, he slid inside to retrieve the bag without a word. Just within the entrance, I hovered, watching the water for fear of the Vetorians and painfully aware of Zeke behind me.

Seconds passed. Besides a few scattered fish in the distance, the ocean near the cave was empty.

The bag slung over his shoulder, Zeke came back toward me.

"Here," he said, tugging out the sieranchine.

I took the jar and scooped out a small amount. My skin tingled with the contact, and when the gel touched my scales, the sensation spread. The pain of the knife slice lessened while, beneath the glistening medicine, the edges of the cut drew together, becoming only a thin line on my tail.

Wordlessly, I handed the jar back to him. He applied a bit to his chest and then returned the medicine to the bag.

From the corner of my eye, I watched the wound on his chest fade, and then I dragged my gaze back to the sea. It was hard to be here, only inches from him again with the adrenaline of the past several minutes gone. I wanted to reach out and touch him.

I wanted him to go away.

"So," Zeke started, his voice tight. He took a breath and glanced around, the motion putting more distance between us. "Where do you want to go now?"

My brow furrowed as I tried to focus. I hadn't really thought about it.

"I... I have a friend who might still be in Santa Lucina."

"Santa Lucina?"

I nodded. "Yeah. Baylie. She's Noah's stepsister." Worry flickered through me. I pressed on. "But she... she won't be like him. We've been friends since we were four. She's from Reidsburg too."

"Does she know about all this?"

I paused. "No."

Unless Noah had said something.

And God knew what he would have told her.

Pain moved through me at the thought that less than an hour ago, Noah talking to Baylie never would have been something to fear. At least, not in this way. He'd talked to his stepmom and brother, after all, and they'd seemed so fine with everything. Supportive. Understanding.

Just like him.

I drew a breath, pushing the hurt away. It didn't matter. I'd made a mistake, trusting him. I'd made a mistake a few minutes ago with Zeke, and I'd made a mistake ever leaving Reidsburg as well. This whole thing was a mess from beginning to end, and now I just needed to get out of here, go back to Kansas, and start over again.

Or something.

"It'll be okay," I continued determinedly, praying I was right. "I'll come up with an explanation."

He didn't answer for a moment. "You can't go back to that house."

I hesitated. "So I'll call her from somewhere. Ask her to come pick me up and drive me out of town right away."

Zeke's face tightened.

"She'll do it," I pressed, not remotely sure if that was true but hoping he'd believe me anyway.

I needed to get out of here.

Zeke sighed. "Alright."

A heartbeat passed.

He swam out of the cave.

Closing my eyes, I took a deep breath and then followed him.

The tide pulled at us as we approached the coast, and beyond its rushing, I could hear the distant sounds of laughter and people splashing in the water. Bright sunlight shone through the waves, making me feel painfully exposed after the darkness of the deeper ocean.

And a few yards away, Zeke swam.

We'd barely spoken in the time it had taken us to return to shore. We'd hardly even come within a dozen feet of each other. I couldn't bring myself to look at him for long, and when I did, discomfort drove me to put even more space between us.

This wasn't how I'd wanted to say goodbye. I didn't really know *what* I'd wanted – I hadn't thought that far ahead – but whatever it had been, this wasn't it.

"Chloe," Zeke said.

I drew a sharp breath, his voice snapping me from my thoughts. I looked back.

His tail was gone and dark swim trunks had taken its place. His eyebrow rose.

Irritation made me grimace, while embarrassment took the opportunity to turn my face red. All this time worrying about people finding out what I was, about them looking at me like a freak, and my own distraction nearly made me swim into the midst of a bunch of strangers in full dehaian form.

Brilliant.

A shiver ran through me as my legs returned and the healing knife cut became a thin red line down the side of my right calf. My scales melted away, leaving only an iridescent and vaguely scale-like swimsuit. Zeke's gaze lingered on me as I changed, and my embarrassment turned to frustration as I looked away.

He was *not* making this easy.

Though given the way he'd been holding me, I didn't know whether he wanted to.

Shivers spread through me for an entirely different reason, and forcibly, I shoved the memories aside. We were coming up on humans. I needed to focus.

The seafloor rose into view as we continued on. Ahead, I could see swimmers' legs kicking to keep them afloat, while surfboards cut through the waves closer by. Ducking low, we gave them a wide berth as we headed for a spot a few hundred yards away. Keeping an eye to the swimmers, we swam onward till the ground sloped up to meet us and the water became too shallow.

Reluctantly, I let my head break the surface. The air took only a moment to become breathable and the burning on my skin passed quickly as well. Just a few people occupied the sand ahead of us, though farther to my left, it was a different story. Children shouted and ran along the beach, while dozens of sunbathers lay on towels beneath the bright summer sun.

I swallowed, hoping no one questioned how we'd suddenly come from the water, or why Zeke had a bag hanging from his shoulder.

"Where are we?" I murmured to him as we walked toward the shore.

"Mariposa Beach," he answered, his voice equally low. "About twenty miles from that guy's house."

We left the waves. Hot sand scorched my feet for less than a heartbeat before a shiver went through me and the pain faded.

I glanced down at my feet. Nothing visible had changed.

We headed through the crowds. A cluster of kids sped past us, racing for the water with their parents jogging behind, while a group of guys played Frisbee nearby. A lifeguard sat in a watchtower several hundred yards off, his attention thankfully focused on a group of swimmers some distance away.

"Over here," Zeke said quietly.

I followed him toward a trio of blonde girls sunbathing on red-striped beach towels.

"Hey," Zeke called to them. "Sorry to bother you, but would you happen to have a cell phone we could borrow?" He gestured to the dripping bag hanging from his shoulder with a chagrinned expression. "Mine sort of took a bath."

Squinting in the bright sunlight, the nearest girl propped herself up on her elbow and then shielded her eyes with a hand. "What?"

"A cell phone. Could we borrow one? It'll only take a second. She just needs to call our ride."

He nodded to me. The girl looked between us and then glanced to her friends.

"Uh, okay," she allowed. "Sure."

She reached over and fumbled her cell from her bag. Extending it to him, she studied him cautiously.

"Thanks," Zeke said, taking the phone and then handing it to me.

We retreated till a few yards separated us from the girls.

Her gaze tracked us.

I swallowed uncomfortably and then dialed Baylie's number. Moments passed while it rang.

"Hello?"

"Baylie?" I let out a breath, nervous and relieved to hear her voice at the same time. "It's Chloe."

Silence answered me.

"Baylie? Are you there?"

"Uh, yeah. Hey, Sandra. What's up?"

My brow drew down in alarm at her stepmother's name. "Sandra? It's—"

She laughed, the sound tight and forced. "That's great. Listen, I can't really talk right now. What did you need?"

I paused. "Are you okay?" I asked carefully.

A heartbeat passed. "Sorry, the connection's bad. What'd you need?"

I hesitated. "A ride."

She didn't respond.

"Baylie? Baylie, please. What's going on?"

She gave a small chuckle, the sound even more forced than before. Rustling came from the other end, like she was moving. "And, uh, where was that again?"

I exhaled. Several feet away, Zeke watched me, his body practically radiating caution.

"Mariposa Beach." I glanced around, looking for a landmark. "Maybe a half mile from a pier. Baylie–"

A nervous cough came from the other end of the line, cutting me off. "Okay, well, uh... yeah." The laugh returned, the noise so unlike her that it made my skin crawl. "Look, I, uh..." The rustling sounded again. "I've got to run, but I'll get you those souvenirs I promised just as soon as I can, alright? Bye."

The line went dead.

I lowered the phone.

"What happened?" Zeke asked warily.

I shook my head. Glancing to the girls on the beach towels, I pushed a smile onto my face and then walked over to them.

"Thanks," I told the blonde girl, handing her the phone.

She nodded.

I turned away, heading back toward Zeke.

"Chloe?" he pressed.

I continued walking. "Something's wrong."

"Wrong how?"

I shook my head. "I don't know."

My brow furrowed as I dropped my gaze to the sand. She'd said she couldn't talk. She hadn't wanted anyone to know it was me.

"Was that guy there?" Zeke asked.

I blinked and glanced to him.

His eyebrow twitched up.

I looked away, my stomach churning at the way he'd put words to my fear. But Noah wouldn't hurt her. At worst – really, *stupidly* worst – he'd only be mad she was speaking to me.

Though that was completely deranged. He couldn't keep Baylie from talking to her friends.

Even if they *were* 'scaly, scum-sucking fish'.

Anger shivered through me at the memory of his words.

"Did she say she was coming to get you?"

Distantly, I nodded.

"Did he hear that?"

I didn't answer, staring unseeing at the cars in the crowded parking lot. This was dumb. Noah may have decided he hated me, though God knew why, but he wasn't a monster.

At least, not that kind of monster.

"Chloe?"

Blinking, I looked to Zeke and shook my head. "I-I don't know."

His mouth tightened. "We need to get out of here," he

said flatly.

I grimaced.

"Chloe, we can't risk–"

He cut off as a young couple strolled past us.

"We don't have a choice," I replied, keeping my voice low as the couple walked away. "I need to get away from the ocean, Zeke. Baylie's my best shot. She knows where I am, she has a car, and she said she'd get here just as soon as she could."

Frustration twisted his face. "And maybe he'll follow her."

I looked away. There was that chance, ridiculous as it was.

But I'd already disappeared on her once before. I'd promised I wouldn't, that night I came back on a bus after my distance from the ocean had nearly driven me insane. But I had.

And the water wasn't safe either. The ghost of a knife slice on my leg proved that.

Zeke sighed. I glanced over at him.

"Or we could watch for her," he relented, though he sounded grudging about it. "Make sure."

A grateful smile pulled at my lip.

He shook his head at the expression. "From someplace a little more out of sight, though," he insisted with a dark glance to the crowds.

I nodded.

Still looking reluctant, he turned and led the way from the beach.

21

NOAH

Footsteps pounded on the stairs. I glanced away from the book I couldn't remember a moment of reading.

Baylie rounded the landing and then ducked into my bedroom. "Can I talk to you?" she whispered.

My brow drew down. It'd been days since she'd wanted to be in the same room with me, let alone talk. Cautiously, I set the book aside and swung my legs off my bed. "What is it?"

She cast a nervous glance over her shoulder and then shut the door. "Chloe just called."

I froze, my blood pressure spiking. "Is she alright?"

Baylie nodded. "I-I think so."

Remembering how to breathe, I dropped my gaze to the floor as my senses stretched out, searching for the other greliarans in the house.

Everyone was downstairs. Maddox was in the kitchen. Dad was on the patio with Richard. And my cousins...

"She needed a ride," Baylie continued.

"Was anyone around when she said that?" I asked distantly, focused on the four of them. They were all together, in the front room from the feel of it, and that was worrisome.

Typically, they stayed spread out at the back of the house to keep a better watch for dehaians.

Baylie made a negative noise. "I stayed as far from everybody as I could and didn't let on that she'd called. I don't think anyone heard."

I hoped she was right.

And I wondered why in the world Chloe wanted a ride.

"Noah..."

I looked back up at Baylie.

"What's going *on?*" she asked, desperation in her blue eyes. "I know the... the thing about you, Maddox, and Peter. But Diane, she wouldn't tell me anything about Chloe. She only said Chloe was involved with that somehow, and wasn't missing like you guys told the cops. She just had to go away for a while."

I tried not to grimace. Diane and her respect for people's privacy. It was wonderful most of the time.

Except for ones like right now.

"But," Baylie continued, "she also said that these cousins and uncle of yours... she told me to stay away from them. Made me swear not to say a word about Chloe around them either, like maybe they're a danger to her or something. I don't understand what's happening, Noah. You're..." She searched for a term and failed. "And then there's these other people no one seems to want around. My best friend's disappeared and nobody will tell me why, even though they swear she's okay. And now she just calls from Marip–"

I rose quickly, holding up a hand to silence her. She flinched back, a terrified look on her face like she thought I'd do something to her.

It made me feel sick.

"Please, Baylie. Don't say where she is."

She nodded jerkily.

I let out a breath, checking downstairs again. No one had moved, and thus they probably hadn't heard.

Hopefully.

"Look," I tried, refocusing. "I swear to you that you're safe around me, alright? I would never, in all my life, *ever* hurt you. And neither would Maddox or Dad. We're still the same people we've always been. So please. *Please* try to believe I'm not a monster?"

She made a desperate noise. "I don't–"

I stepped forward and she flinched again.

Chagrin colored her face.

"Sorry," she whispered.

I nodded.

"It's just..."

"Weird," I finished for her.

"Scary."

I wasn't sure what to say.

"Does it... you know, hurt?" she asked.

I hesitated and then shook my head.

She drew an unsteady breath. "Is Chloe like you?"

For a heartbeat, I searched for a response. Chloe had been so worried about telling Baylie the truth, and after how things had gone the past few days, I couldn't blame her. Sure, finding out nearly everyone around you wasn't human wasn't easy. But I didn't want Baylie to look at Chloe the way she'd been looking at me for the last week. Chloe'd had enough trouble with how people treated her today.

And maybe this was her secret to share.

"No."

"So why–"

"Baylie, she's not. She's just... she's your friend. And..."

I hesitated, wishing I could do more than this. Be the one to go find her, even if I knew the odds of me getting away from my cousins were small.

"And she needs your help," I continued. "So you go pick her up and whatever you do, don't bring her back here. Just get her in the car and take her wherever she needs to go. And if you're heading away from the ocean and she tells you to stop, you have to, alright? No matter what."

She stared at me like I was insane.

"Please," I begged her.

Questions rose in her eyes, but after a heartbeat, they died. "Okay," she agreed uncertainly.

"Thank you."

She nodded.

I drew a breath. "Alright. Head downstairs and I'll try to distract–"

All four cousins vanished from my awareness.

A curse escaped me. Baylie stumbled aside as I tore across the room and yanked open the door.

I made it to the base of the stairs and found Wyatt leaning on the open doorway with his brothers by the car in the driveway beyond.

"Problem, cuz?" he asked mildly.

I shivered. He looked like a cat with a canary, if that cat was the size of a several-hundred-pound weightlifter.

And more bloodthirsty.

"What are you–"

"Oh, we just wanted your attention," Wyatt replied. He glanced to Baylie. "Doesn't help to go in the other room, girl. We can still hear you." He winked at her and then returned his attention to me. "And now we're going fishing."

Owen grinned and then climbed into the car.

I shoved past Wyatt, heading for him.

Clay stepped into my path as the engine started. Cracks tried to spread through my skin as he grabbed me, and only the fact we were in view of the neighborhood kept me from letting them spread farther.

Baylie shrieked. I looked over my shoulder to see Wyatt snag her arm and yank her to him.

"Hey!" Maddox shouted from deeper in the house. I could feel him running toward us as I shoved at Clay, fighting to break his grip.

Wyatt muscled Baylie forward, driving her down the stairs at his side. Desperately, she swung a fist at him.

He paid it no attention.

"Take her!" he yelled at Brock, and shoved Baylie to him.

Brock caught her as she stumbled, and he swiftly wrenched her arm behind her back. She cried out with pain as he propelled her ahead of him toward the car.

"What do you think?" Wyatt called to me. "Nice bait, eh?"

Ignoring him, I twisted in Clay's grasp and then slammed an elbow into his side. He choked, his grip loosening.

I ran for Baylie.

In the car, Owen twisted in his seat and threw open the rear door. Brock forced her toward the vehicle.

I swung a fist at his head.

Brock staggered, his hold on Baylie breaking. She tumbled to the ground.

Clay grabbed me, pulling me backward. I turned, spotting Maddox at the base of the porch steps, his arms pinning both of Wyatt's to keep him from following.

"Hey!" Dad shouted. He rushed outside. "Break it up!"

He shoved Maddox and Wyatt apart and then stormed toward us. Behind him, Richard strolled onto the porch, his gaze taking in his sons, the car, and Baylie on the ground with one unconcerned sweep.

"What the hell is this?" Dad demanded, helping Baylie to her feet.

"Ask them," I snapped, jerking my head toward Owen and Brock by the car. "They're the ones who just tried to kidnap Baylie."

"Now, hang on," Richard interjected. "Who says they were *kidnapping* her?"

"Them," Baylie said. She looked up at my dad. "They called me bait."

Dad paused, studying her. Marks showed on her arms, red and vivid and promising deep bruises to come, while her palms were scraped and bloodied from the fall to the driveway.

And his face darkened.

"Is this true?" he asked them.

I swallowed, recognizing the dangerously low tone.

Even if my cousins didn't.

Wyatt scoffed. "Come on, Uncle Peter. That thing is waiting for her! Maybe others are too. If we put this girl out there, who knows how many we might–"

Dad strode toward him. Wyatt's eyes went wide and he retreated a step.

"Peter," Richard started.

"You were going to use Baylie as *bait*?" Dad snapped. "For *them*?"

Wyatt blanched. "I–"

"Get out," Dad snarled. "All of you. I brought you here to keep my family protected, and if you…" He shook his head. I could see him fighting to keep control. "You're done. Go home. Now."

"Wait a minute," Richard protested, descending the stairs. "Now, my boys wouldn't have put the girl in any real danger. She was just being stubborn about her friend. And besides, those creatures are still out there. You can't honestly expect us to just leave them be, when they're–"

"Enough!" Dad ordered. Muscles jumped in his jaw. "Enough, Richard. Go home."

Richard watched him for a moment. Contempt twitched his lip. "Coward."

He jerked his chin at his sons. "Let's go." He turned to head back inside.

Wyatt stared at him. "You can't be serious. They're–"

"You heard me," Richard retorted.

"No!" Wyatt shouted. "No, you're not..."

He exhaled sharply and ran for the car.

"Wyatt!" his father yelled.

I moved to intercept him.

Clay grabbed me and spun, trying to toss me aside. I stumbled and then threw an elbow back, hitting his midsection.

The car door slammed. Owen hit the gas.

He and Wyatt sped away.

Clay chuckled. I turned as he stepped back, holding up his hands with a smirk.

I slammed my fist into his face.

"Hey!" Richard barked as his son staggered.

I ignored him, looking to Baylie. "Where is she? Where'd she ask you to meet her?"

"M-Mariposa Beach."

"Noah!" Maddox called.

I glanced over and then caught his keys from the air.

"Hold on!" Dad snapped, starting toward me.

I ran for Maddox's car.

Behind me, I could feel Clay trying to catch up, with Dad close behind. From the porch, Richard yelled protests, while Maddox kept Brock from joining the chase.

The key fob nearly broke under my thumb. The locks on Maddox's sports car popped up.

I swung inside and slammed the door. Clay grabbed at the handle. He snarled at finding it locked, and then raised an arm to smash through the glass.

The ignition turned over. I crushed the pedal to the floor as his arm swung, and the car surged forward, leaving him stumbling.

I raced from the driveway.

22

CHLOE

On a secluded park bench at the edge of the sand, we sat surrounded by bushes and watched the crowds of people.

Who made me feel like they were staring at us, even when I knew they weren't.

I wasn't sure how fast Baylie would get here – if she'd needed a cover story to leave, that could take some time – but as the minutes crept past, I could feel my anxiety building. Whether or not it'd been Noah she'd worried about, Baylie had still tried to hide the fact she was speaking to me. I didn't know what that could mean, but it couldn't be a good sign.

And meanwhile, the whole ocean lay in front of us, filled with people who'd tried to hurt me and Zeke in one way or another.

I swallowed, watching the waves roll in. Those people weren't psychic, however. They wouldn't just magically know that, out of all the miles and miles of coastline on the Earth, we were sitting here.

Drawing a shaky breath, I twisted on the bench to look back at the busy street and tried to make myself believe the words.

"You alright?" Zeke asked quietly.

I glanced to him. His face tight, he didn't look at me, but kept his gaze on the crowd on the beach.

"Fine," I replied, turning my attention back to the road.

A minute crawled by.

"Chloe, if she doesn't show–"

"She will."

My gaze flicked to him, and then returned to the street. Somewhere between a city road and a scenic highway, the wide thoroughfare bordered the beach parking lot and was filled with everything from convertibles to minivans rushing along in either direction.

But not her car.

"What the–" Zeke began.

I turned as he rose to his feet, his eyes locked on the beach. Heart racing, I followed his gaze.

Niall was walking at the edge of the tide.

A breath left Zeke. He started forward and then paused, throwing a quick look back as though torn between going toward his brother and staying by me.

I got up and followed him down to the sand, scanning the area as I went. Niall caught sight of us as we came closer.

He grinned with relief. "*There* you are. We've been–" He glanced to the crowds and tossed a nod at someone there.

"We've been looking all over."

"What are you doing here?" Zeke asked. "Are you okay?"

"Fine. Woke up a few hours ago. Jirral told me where you were headed and," he shrugged, "we've been looking ever since."

I glanced over as several men walked up, something in their stance and eyes giving them away as dehaian. They nodded to Niall, and then took up positions near us and returned their attention to the crowds.

"Are you guys alright?" Niall continued. "What are you doing out here like this?"

Zeke twitched his head toward me. "She's got a friend coming to pick her up."

Niall paused. "Zeke, this place is..." He lowered his voice as several kids ran by. "Damn, I mean, it's *crawling* with mercenaries. I don't even know how you missed them to get here."

"We didn't."

Niall's brow furrowed and then he seemed to see the thin line from the knife slice on Zeke's chest. He blinked. "Look," he managed, "you need to come back home. Both of you. Ren–"

Zeke shook his head. "No way. Not with what happened to her last time we were there. She needs to get out of here, Niall. There's no other option."

"But that's the thing." Niall let out a breath in a tight chuckle. "Ren, um... he believes you. About her, and the–" A pair of surfers jogged past. "The Sylphaen."

"He does?"

Niall nodded. "He *found* Liana, Zeke. Or, I mean, his soldiers did. Found her a few miles north of Nyciena. She was swimming like hell from something, and didn't even spot them till it was too late. She cracked, though. Told him everything after he... well, he's Ren. You know how much of a jackass he can be when he wants something."

I shifted uncomfortably at the words, and Niall gave me a sympathetic look.

"And he doesn't still think Chloe was involved?" Zeke pressed.

"Not after Liana started spouting off crazy shit, talking about Chloe being some 'abomination' thing. Real end-of-the-world type stuff. Finally got the truth through even *his* thick head."

I shivered, though from memories of the Sylphaen's babble or the possibility Ren finally believed I wasn't a spy, I didn't know. But I looked to Zeke, and I could see the cautious hope in his eyes.

He wanted us to go back, I could tell.

Nervously, I bit my lip. This was great for him. Wonderful, really.

But spies could still be there. They could still try to hurt what family Zeke had left.

I shook my head at the look in his eyes. His brow drew down.

"There could be more out there," I reminded him quietly.

"And there are hundreds of soldiers on alert now. They won't–"

"You don't know that."

A breath left him and he looked away. His brow furrowed. "You don't belong back there, Chloe."

"Zeke, I have to–"

"You don't."

I grimaced and turned my gaze away, unable to meet his eyes.

Niall glanced between us. "We need to get moving. Like I said, those guys are everywhere around here."

I nodded. "You both should, yeah."

Zeke scowled. "I'm not leaving you here."

Frustration rose in me. "I can't–"

"He's right," Niall interjected. "Chloe, what are you going to do if those Sylphaen guys are following your friend? They'll probably leave anyone else alone if you're not around – I mean, they don't care about them, right? But if you're there, and it's just you two on the highway somewhere…"

Worry clouded his eyes.

I looked away.

"You'll do your friend more good keeping them out of this," Niall finished. "And Zeke's right. Home is safer. Ren… well, you might've noticed he's a bit territorial. If he thinks you matter to our family," he glanced to Zeke briefly, "he'll keep you safe."

The grimace returned to my face. I couldn't do this to Baylie. Not again. I'd disappeared only a few days ago, when I'd left with the dehaians rather than go back to land.

That hadn't been my choice. But this was.

"I know this is hard, Chloe," Niall said. "But–"

"They could kill her," Zeke finished quietly. "You know that too."

I hesitated, my gaze flicking to him while my mind tossed up recollections of what those psychos had done to other girls in their efforts to find me. Shivering, I tried to push the thought away.

It wouldn't go.

"Please," Zeke pressed. "You–"

"Okay," I snapped.

I looked away. I knew they were right. It hurt and it sucked, but I knew they were right.

Zeke seemed to release the breath he'd been holding. He glanced to Niall. "How do we want to–"

Tires squealed in the parking lot, followed immediately by a sickening crunch of metal. We spun to see a light pole lurch sideways, while screams rose past the rows of parked cars.

I started forward. Zeke snagged my arm.

Panicked, I looked back at him.

"If it's them," he hissed.

Zeke twitched his chin at the guards. "Go. Check if there's a girl in the cars."

Two of the guards nodded and then ran toward the accident.

I shrugged off Zeke's arm, my gaze on the parking lot. But even by letting my eyes change a bit and risking the faint glow that came with my sharpened vision, I couldn't tell much past the glare of the sunlight and the lines of parked cars.

Seconds ticked by.

"We need to get going..." Niall urged in a low tone.

I shook my head, not looking away from what little I could see of the accident. "Not yet."

He made a frustrated sound. I ignored him, my heart pounding while I watched to see if anyone climbed from the vehicles. Sirens rose in the distance, racing closer.

The guards came back.

"No girl in either car," one of them reported quietly, keeping an eye to the beachgoers around us.

I swallowed. "What about the guys, then? What did they look like?"

"Chloe," Zeke started.

"If Noah was–"

"We need to go," Niall interrupted. "Zeke, if the Sylphaen are around..."

"Come on," Zeke said to me, reaching out to take my arm again.

I jerked away.

His mouth tightened. "Please, Chloe. This is going to attract attention, regardless. We don't want anyone spotting us standing here."

For a heartbeat, I stared at him, wanting to argue even

though I knew he had a point.

"Fine."

Niall glanced to the guards. "Meet up in twenty, eh?"

They nodded. All but two of them walked away.

"Come on," Zeke said to me.

With a last look to the accident, I followed him in the opposite direction of the other guards. We walked down the shoreline until finally we reached a place not far from where Zeke and I had first arrived.

Niall gave me a grin and then headed into the water. Swimming away from the shore, he continued along for a few minutes, and then suddenly dove beneath the waves.

Zeke glanced back the way we'd come. Confused, I followed his gaze.

From his tower, a muscled young man scanned the water, a yellow life-preserver stashed by his side.

But for the moment, he was looking in the other direction.

Zeke waited a heartbeat more, watching the young man check toward us and then return his gaze to the crowd ahead.

I followed Zeke into the water.

A quiver ran through me at the touch of the waves, and I took a quick breath, concentrating on not letting my skin change. As the water deepened, we began swimming through the tide that kept trying to push us back toward the shore.

Zeke made a small noise of approval. I glanced back.

On the beach, a police officer was walking toward the lifeguard. Calling out to the young man, he motioned to the parking lot as though asking a question.

The lifeguard turned, looking toward the accident.

"Go," Zeke said.

We dove beneath the water.

My lungs adjusted instantly and my skin trembled with the urge to change. Holding onto mostly human form, I trailed Zeke deeper into the water, my ears still attuned for shouts of alarm from the coast behind us.

But none came. Splashing of swimmers and the rush of the waves were the only sounds.

The seafloor descended. The change shivered through me a heartbeat after it raced through him.

We took off, leaving Santa Lucina behind.

23

NOAH

Through the shattered windshield and the crowds, I watched Chloe walk into the ocean.

And I swore.

I wanted to go to her and explain what had happened, now that my cousins couldn't reach her, but the door was solidly jammed, the steering wheel had come down to pin my legs, and short of going greliaran on them both and scaring the hell out of the people surrounding the car, I had no way out.

She glanced back to the shore for a heartbeat, her auburn hair shining in the brilliant sunlight, and then she dove beneath the water.

I slammed a hand into the dashboard, denting the plastic in my frustration.

It'd taken me minutes on end to catch up to Owen and Wyatt, despite racing through stop signs and stoplights and praying that the cops wouldn't see. My cousins had already arrived at the lot by the time I got here, and if not for the fact they'd parked at the end of a row of cars, I would have had almost no chance of stopping them.

And Chloe had been standing on the sand.

There hadn't been many options. I couldn't take them both on and be certain one of them wouldn't slip away to reach her.

I just hoped Maddox would forgive me about his car.

Waves crashed in and rolled back out again. No fins or scales broke the surface, and on the beach, no one shouted or pointed to the space where the dehaians had disappeared.

The accident had distracted them.

Someone knocked on the window of the car, and I pulled my gaze from the water to find a cop staring down at me. Up ahead, Wyatt shouted curses, barely keeping himself from losing control in his rage. Next to him, Owen resorted to a glare, though I knew he'd try more once he could leave the driver's seat.

Which, considering they were trapped between Maddox's car and a light pole, would be a while.

The cop motioned to other officers farther in the crowd. Past the cars around me, I saw an ambulance pull into the lot.

I sighed. There'd be hell to pay for this. But Chloe was safe. From my family, at least, she was safe.

And that was the best I could do.

⌒ 24 ⌒

CHLOE

After a few miles, we met up with Niall, and several miles after that came the guards. Watchful and silent, the men surrounded us, their attention on the possibility of attack and their path taking us back toward Nyciena. Neither of the brothers spoke as we continued on, time ticking by till finally we reached a patch of boulders on the seafloor and Niall murmured for the guards to stop.

Both of them waited till the guards had set a veil around us before ever saying a word.

"So what's Ren planning to do to Liana?" Zeke asked quietly as he shrugged off the bag and left it sitting on the sand. A small fire burned blue in front of us, casting light on the boulders inside the veil but strangely doing nothing to those beyond.

Across the flames, Niall glanced up. "What do you think?"

Zeke's gaze flicked to me and then away. "Did she say anything about others? The Sylphaen elsewhere?"

Niall paused. "Not yet."

Zeke nodded.

Silence returned.

I looked between them, not wanting to break it. It felt weird to be swimming back to Nyciena again. Almost like déjà vu of our trip a few days before, if not for the weight of everything that'd happened in between.

And the questions of what would happen now. I felt like a yo-yo, being thrust away from one location and then yanked back again. I'd had no choice about traveling to Nyciena a week ago. Then I'd had no choice but to leave there and return to Santa Lucina. I'd tried to find a way back to land *twice* only to be driven to the ocean again, and now...

Now I didn't know what to feel anymore.

Zeke shifted a bit on the sand, and my gaze didn't quite twitch his way.

Especially when it came to him.

"So what about you?" Zeke said to Niall. "You alright?"

A hint of Niall's old humor ghosted across his face, though it seemed mostly bitter. "Yeah."

"What happened?" I asked when he didn't say any more.

He hesitated. "Kyne thinks it was something we ate. Time release poison in our food or something. And maybe... I don't know. Maybe since Ren and I didn't have the same stuff sent to our rooms as Dad probably did, or maybe because Liana got the dose wrong..." He trailed off, shaking his head. "It didn't kill us. I don't know."

A moment passed.

Niall took a breath. "So what about you two? You said there were Vetorians?"

Zeke nodded. "Yeah. Not too far from here."

I didn't add anything, and he didn't continue. Niall looked between us. "You guys alright?"

"Fine," Zeke said.

I tried for a smile and mostly failed.

Niall paused. His eyebrow inched up. "You have a fight or something?"

Zeke tossed him an irritated glare. "Niall, we're fine."

His brother's expression didn't change. If anything, it grew more skeptical.

I looked away. I really didn't want to talk about it and I was fairly certain Zeke didn't either. I had no idea what things would be like between us now that I was heading back to Nyciena with him. I didn't even know if it *mattered* what things were like. He... what was he, anyway? A prince, sure. Okay. But what else?

Everyone seemed to think he just slept around, going through girls like firecrackers – fun and pretty and exciting for a bit, but then it was over and he moved on.

I wasn't going to be that for him.

He didn't seem as though he saw me that way.

But then, I'd read enough books and watched enough movies to know that the talented ones, the real users, never did.

Except…

I shifted uncomfortably on the grit of the seafloor, wishing I had about a century to unravel the tangle of my thoughts. Or at least space. Having Zeke so close – and Niall with his blatant curiosity too – was making it hard to think.

"So what happened?" Niall asked.

I looked up in alarm.

"Huh?" Zeke asked, and I could hear the guarded note in his voice.

"That," Niall explained with a twitch of his chin to the cut on Zeke's chest.

"Oh," Zeke said, nodding. "Yeah. A few mercenaries caught us out by the Shiaran Fells." He paused. "It was fine."

Niall's brow inched upward again.

Pushing away from the sand, Zeke didn't look at him. "I'm going to go check on the…"

He seemed to have trouble coming up with something, and then just swam off.

Niall's expression didn't change.

I rose, trying to make a break for it in the other direction before he could press the issue with me.

It only took Niall a heartbeat to catch up.

"Hey," he called.

I stopped a few yards from where I'd been, not turning around.

Niall came up beside me and then glanced back to Zeke on the far end of the camp. "Can I talk to you?" he asked me.

He motioned around the side of a large pile of boulders.

I hesitated, but there wasn't much of an option, short of being rude. Reluctantly, I nodded and followed him.

"Listen," he said when we were out of sight of Zeke. "I know I was sort of almost dead not too long ago, so I might be a bit loopy, but... are you two okay? Really? You both seem... tense. Like something happened. More than a Vetorian attack, I mean. And Zeke's such a... well, I know him. He wouldn't ever tell me."

I hesitated, not wanting to discuss this with Zeke's brother of all people.

Though, to be fair, Ina would have been just as bad.

I pushed the thoughts aside. "We're fine."

He waited.

"Really," I insisted.

He nodded, though he obviously didn't believe me. "Okay..."

A grimace twisted my face as I looked away. Niall wasn't stupid. And apparently I wasn't a very good liar. "It's just, earlier today... Zeke kissed me."

From the corner of my eye, I saw his brow flicker down in confusion.

"Oh, for the... *please* don't tell me you thought we were sleeping together too," I begged tiredly.

"No, of course not."

The answer was too quick. I tried not to groan.

"Well, okay," he acquiesced. "Maybe I figured by *now* he...

Never mind. Look, I'm sorry. Really."

I glanced back at him. He gave me an apologetic smile.

"I swear," he continued. "But honestly, why is that so bad? Zeke's not as handsome as me, I'll give you that. But he's not a monster."

My lip twitched.

He grinned and reached out, taking my hand. "Come on," he pressed. He glanced around, but no one was nearby. "*That's* all this is? Zeke kissed you? I thought maybe it'd been something... I don't know. *Horrible.*" The conciliatory expression on his face vanished. "Like slicing a mercenary's back open."

My breath caught.

His fingers clenched on my hand to halt my startled retreat and he yanked me toward him. His grip twisted, spinning me, and my back slammed up against his chest with his arm at my throat.

Spikes grew from his forearm, aimed at my neck. "Scream and the Beast will be the least of your worries."

My blood went cold.

From behind a rock ahead of us, a woman rose. Gray-haired with faded blue scales, she regarded us with nothing but contempt in her icy eyes. "Took you long enough," she said to Niall.

"Keep it down," Niall growled. "He's just over there."

Her contempt deepened.

With an angry noise, Niall swam toward her, bringing me

along. From her bag, the woman drew out a pair of shackles and then reached for my wrists. I tried to pull away, and Niall's grip tightened, bringing the spikes to rest on my neck.

I froze. The metal clamped down on my forearms. Her lip curling, the woman glanced pointedly from me to the small stone clipped to the glittering belt around her hips and then back again.

A shiver ran through me.

With his free hand, Niall reached past me to grab the thick chain between the manacles, keeping his other arm to my throat. Holding me fast, he moved between the rocks, heading for the edge of the veil.

"Why are you doing this, Niall?" I tried, raising my voice as much as I dared.

"Shut it," he muttered.

Barely breathing, I watched the translucent knives next to my skin. "Please, you don't have to—"

The spikes twitched upward, nicking my cheek. I flinched aside.

"Chloe," he warned, the chilling promise of further retribution in his tone. "Not another sound."

His spikes at my throat, he dragged me through the veil and left the camp behind.

25

ZEKE

I swam over to the guards, not really sure what I was going to say, and when I got there, words steadfastly refused to present themselves.

But then, talking was just an excuse anyway. I'd needed to get away from the campfire. Being near Niall, near Chloe, was harder than I'd expected. It was great that Ren's guys had found Liana. Great that he believed me – *finally* – about Chloe.

Yet nothing was really over. The Sylphaen were still out there. Dad was still dead. And I couldn't shake the fear that they'd come after us again. That whatever they'd wanted – because I couldn't believe for a second this'd *all* just been to capture Chloe – they'd still try to get.

I'd almost lost Niall. Ren too, insufferable ass that he was. Ina and I had probably just escaped by luck. I didn't want to go through all that again.

And I didn't want to risk anyone hurting Chloe either.

Behind me, I heard Niall call out to her, asking to talk, and I kept myself from turning around. I couldn't imagine she'd tell him what happened, though Niall was charming as hell when he wanted to be. And it wasn't important anyway. The minor fact I'd kissed some girl wouldn't exactly be shocking to him.

My stomach twisted at the rancor of the thought. She wasn't just some girl. She hadn't been for a long time, though damn if I could figure out why. But she mattered, in a way that had nothing to do with crazy cults or her strange land-walker heritage.

And when I was around her, I barely knew what to do with myself anymore.

I grimaced, pretending to check the food a guard was preparing simply so I could look busy. She was coming back with us, though. And I wanted that. I'd hated the thought of her leaving, hated it more than I had words to describe, and for her to be returning to Nyciena with us now…

It was great too.

Except for the part where she didn't want to go.

My gaze twitched back toward her. Things would be different this time. She–

She was gone.

And Niall was too.

My brow furrowing, I glanced to the guards. "Hey, did you all see where they went?"

The guards looked to each other, appearing confused.

I swam toward the rest of the campsite. Maybe they'd gone behind the rocks, though why the hell they–

"Your highness?" one of the guards called.

"What?" I replied, not turning around.

The man circled in front of me, cutting me off.

"Hey–"

"We need your assistance," he interrupted.

"With what?"

"The path back to Nyciena. You said you saw Vetorians."

I shook my head, dismissing the implicit questions. "Later," I said, moving to go around him. Why would she and Niall–

"But highness," he countered, staying in front of me.

I stopped, taken aback. "Didn't you hear me, soldier? I said later. Now get out of my way."

His face tightened. He didn't move.

I glanced to the others, but they remained seated by the preparations for food.

"What is this?" I demanded.

No one would respond.

I looked at the man blocking my path. "Answer me."

His gaze went to the others briefly. "Prince Nialloran asked for a moment with the young lady. In private."

My brow twitched down. "What?"

"Apologies, highness. The young lady seemed most… interested in time alone with him. I believe he intends to let her down easy."

My confusion deepened. "Wait, she…" I shook my head.

"Chloe's not…"

"He asked that you not disturb him."

I looked back at the other guards. To a person, they watched me with sympathetic expressions and a hint of readiness to intercept me if I moved to go after Niall.

My gaze dropped to the ground. This didn't make sense. Chloe hadn't shown any interest in my brother. She'd hardly even *mentioned* Niall, except to ask if he and Ina were alright.

Though maybe that'd been more than just polite concern for him. Maybe she'd actually…

I shoved the thought aside. Bullshit. Chloe never gave one sign of that, and I was pretty damn good at reading women. If she'd been into Niall, I would have seen *something*.

And regardless, I wasn't going to let some guard say Chloe had lied to me this entire time and let that be it.

I looked back up.

"Huh," I commented, barely keeping the fury from my tone. "Hopefully not too easy, eh?"

Disgust tugging at my face, I started to turn away.

The guard relaxed and moved to follow me.

I twisted and kicked hard in the water. With a startled cry, he grabbed for me as I shot past.

He missed.

I rocketed across the camp, scanning the area as I went. I couldn't pick up any sign of them close by, and as I whipped around the boulders on the far side, they weren't there either.

But they wouldn't have left camp. There wasn't any reason

for that.

Unless he'd changed his mind. Unless she'd wanted some privacy…

I shook off the thought. The guards were coming.

Spinning, I darted past the veil and sped away from the campsite. Murky twilight surrounded me, blue and endless with only rocks to break the monotony. There was hardly any life in this place and even the current seemed still compared to the tides we'd left behind.

Three forms tickled the edge of my senses far ahead, too small to be sharks and too fast as well.

A breath left me and my heart began pounding harder. Three people, not two. Whatever the guards' stories, this couldn't be good.

Fighting for every bit of speed I could get, I raced after them.

26

CHLOE

Water rushed in my ears as Niall dragged me along, and up ahead, the gray-haired woman never looked back.

I drew shallow breaths, my eyes on the spikes next to my face and my hands twisting in the shackles holding my forearms. I didn't know what to do. Zeke's brother was a Sylphaen. He was undoubtedly taking me to more of them.

And I didn't know what to do.

"Zeke's going to come after us," I tried. "How are you going to expl–"

Niall's grip on my chest tightened, choking off my words.

"I'm not your enemy, Niall," I managed. "Please, I–"

In the water, the woman turned like an eel. I caught a glimpse of the weathered and opaque spikes on her arm, and then she shot past and slashed them across my chest.

Pain raced through me, delayed by shock but only for a heartbeat. Blood clouded the water, streaming away from me as we flew along. Gasping, I looked down to see slices across my chest.

They weren't deep. Barely more than paper cuts. They might not even scar.

But oh, they hurt.

"Liana!" Niall snapped.

The woman ignored him. "Wisdom Kirzan wants you weakened," she said to me. "It's up to you how weak that will be."

Breathing in short gasps, I stared at her.

Contempt narrowed her eyes, and then she continued on ahead.

"You bleed her too much before the ceremony, Kirzan will make an example of you the way he did with that idiot, Jesse," Niall threatened her.

The name of the bookstore clerk pulled me from my shock.

"And if she stays strong enough to draw it to her before we're ready, what then?" Liana tossed back.

At his silence, she snorted with disgust. "You just keep her under control and let me worry about the Wisdom."

Niall growled something under his breath that even I couldn't make out. Tightening his grip on me, he continued after the woman.

I swallowed down a breath, trying to ignore the sting of the cuts on my scales. Jesse. Wisdom something or other. The EMTs who'd attacked me had mentioned 'the Wisdom' too.

Panic made it hard to keep breathing. I had to get out of here.

My hands twisted in the manacles. If I made a break for it, these things would electrocute me with a single touch to the device at Liana's belt. It was miles back to the campsite, with nowhere to hide and no help in between. But we were moving toward a range of low hills and pockmark caves on the seafloor, and it didn't take a genius to know I was running out of time.

A form appeared at the edge of my senses behind us. And it was racing this way.

I choked down another breath, praying it was Zeke or someone else *not* Sylphaen.

Niall glanced over his shoulder, the motion bringing his spikes closer to my face. I leaned away, pulling at his grip, but his muscular arm didn't budge.

The tiny form sped closer, moving so fast it could only be dehaian.

Niall muttered a vehement curse. He looked to Liana.

"Down there," she ordered.

He dove, bringing me in tow. Caves on the slopes of the hills passed beneath us, till he darted toward a large opening and followed Liana inside.

Darkness surrounded us.

"One sound…" Niall murmured, his spikes resting on my cheek again.

I trembled.

Over the tops of the hills, the dehaian swam closer and then slowed, as though searching for where we'd gone.

Hope made my breath catch. Zeke. Even if I couldn't see

him through the twilight of the water, I knew it was him.

My gaze twitched to the spikes touching my face. Niall couldn't kill me. I'd thought he would, but they needed me for something first. He'd made that clear to Liana when she cut me.

He could still scar me horribly.

But he couldn't actually *kill* me. Not until we reached wherever they were going, anyway. Then, I was definitely dead.

My heart racing, I drew a sharp breath and then twisted sideways and swung my elbow at his midsection.

The spikes slipped backward as he choked, the tips narrowly missing my face.

"Zeke!" I screamed, struggling to break free of Niall's grasp. "Zeke, down–"

Liana's fist hit my stomach, doubling me over, and then Niall's free hand grasped my hair and yanked me back upright. I started to shriek, when his other hand clamped down on my mouth.

But I could feel Zeke diving toward us.

Liana's face twitched with a silent snarl. She jerked her chin at Niall.

With his arm around my chest again and his hand on my mouth, he hauled me toward the rear of the cave, Liana coming after us. Large rocks hulked in the shadows, and quickly, Niall ducked behind them, dragging me down with him.

Seconds passed. I could feel his rapid breathing where my

back pressed to his chest.

"Who's in there?" Zeke called from the entrance, cold threat in his voice.

On my mouth, Niall's hand quivered. From the corner of my eye, I saw him glance to Liana.

Spikes slid from her forearms. Fury flashed across Niall's face as he shook his head.

Her lip curled disgustedly.

"Niall?" Zeke continued.

I felt a breath leave Niall and his muscles twitched as though barely restraining a curse. With a dark glance to Liana, he jerked his head to me and then toward Zeke.

The woman nodded. She braced her arm across my chest, aiming her spikes at my throat, while with her free hand, she clamped her palm to my mouth.

Niall slid out from behind me. Liana pressed me backward till I bumped into the rock. The tips of her spikes hovered so close, they brushed my neck with every breath.

From behind the boulders, Niall straightened.

"Zeke..." he said, sounding breathless and relieved. "No! Don't come closer." He paused. "They have Chloe behind me. If you don't leave..."

I tried to pull away from Liana's grip. Her nails dug into my cheek as her hold on my mouth tightened.

"What happened, Niall?" Zeke asked warily.

"Please," his brother begged. "You have to go. I can handle this. Just—"

"Sure. Okay."

My brow furrowed incredulously. I looked over, the edge of my gaze catching Niall.

He didn't move, but I could see relief creeping through his posture.

"But one thing?" Zeke offered carefully. "Remember how they need her for some kind of sacrifice?"

Niall paused. I glanced to Liana. Her eyes were locked on Niall, her expression visibly willing him to attack Zeke and get it over with.

I trembled. My gaze dropped to the spikes at my throat, and then caught on the stone clipped to her belt.

"She's no good to them dead," Zeke continued. "Not yet."

"Zeke, please," Niall tried. "Back off. You're gambling Chloe's life here."

I grabbed the tiny device on Liana's belt and crushed it in my fists.

Pain shot through me like rapid-fire bolts of lightning. The electricity passed from me to her through her grip on my skin and sent her lurching away with a shriek, the motion ripping the stone from my hand.

The lightning vanished. My body sizzling from the jolt, I gasped and twisted away from her.

"He's lying!" I shouted. My tail thrashed in the water as I scrambled around the boulder and tried to swim past Niall. "He's–"

Niall's hand caught my hair. Brutally, he yanked me

backward, and I cried out, my shackled hands instinctively reaching to break his hold.

He shoved them away. His arm went around my shoulders again, the spikes returning and aimed at my throat.

By the cave entrance, Zeke froze.

"Why couldn't you just go?" Niall whispered to him. "I tried to keep you out of this. You and Ina both. Why couldn't you just *go?*"

Zeke didn't respond. Shock and horror seemed to be having trouble deciding which would show on his face first.

From behind the boulders, I heard Liana struggle up, gasping and snarling curses under her breath.

Zeke's gaze twitched to her and then back to his brother. The horror deepened.

"Grab him," Niall ordered her. "Don't hurt him unless you have to."

Liana muttered something as she swam past, her interpretation of necessity clear in the sound.

Zeke retreated, spikes on his arms bringing Liana to a halt. "What... Niall, you..."

"I didn't want this, Zeke. You should have left."

"What are you *doing?* You... Niall..." Zeke's brow drew down, pain in his eyes. "You killed Dad?"

I struggled in Niall's grip. He clenched his arm tighter on me.

"He was in the way," Niall replied, his voice almost dead. "He wouldn't have listened, so he had to be removed in a manner that would never let suspicion fall on me. And Ren needed to think it was an attack. He needed his fears confirmed so he'd make it simple for us to get to her." He paused. "Ren's easy to manipulate, and the country needs to be under our control for what's to come."

A gasp escaped Zeke. He looked from Niall to Liana and then his head twitched, as though he picked up on something in the distance beyond the cave.

Liana started forward. Zeke tensed, his arm moving between them. She stopped.

"Let Chloe go, Niall," he tried. "Please. You don't want to—"

"No."

I winced as his spikes pressed to my neck, the tips piercing my skin.

Zeke shivered, watching us. "Why? Why would you—"

"Because the Sylphaen are right."

Another choked sound left Zeke.

"Our people are weak," Niall continued. "We die for... for what? Being on land? Offending some law of nature, some ancient magic that says we can't leave the water for too long?" His fingers dug into my scalp. "You tell me, Zeke. If there was a way to change that, to change the *hell* that happens to little kids when they get stranded somewhere and can't return home, wouldn't you take it?"

My gaze slid to Niall in confusion.

"I've heard this before," Zeke said, something dark entering his voice.

"Wisdom Kirzan," Niall acknowledged.

"He the one who made you join them?"

"No one *made* me. I saw the truth. The Wisdom visited the west garrison, back when Dad sent me there as punishment for my time with the Lyceran ambassador's daughter, and we talked." He paused. "It makes sense, Zeke, if only you'd try to understand."

"I understand you joined a bunch of psychos who murdered our father! Who want to sacrifice Chloe! *Chloe*, Niall! She's our friend and you–"

"She's an abomination."

"Why?" Zeke cried furiously. "Because she's half-landwalker? So *what*?"

"She's much more than that."

My brow drew down even as Zeke's did the same.

"You already know she can stay on land longer than any of us could dream," Niall told him. "But that's not the half of it. You have no idea what this creature will be capable of. We do. And we're going to take that. Now, before she can stop us."

Zeke stared at him. "Listen to yourself, Niall. *Please*! She's just a girl. You can't do this! You–"

"And you don't know what's coming, Zeke! Her life condemns us all. It already has. You think possessed water attacking her is bad? That's nothing compared to what will happen. The Beast is out there. It's weak now, but it's going to get stronger, and when that happens, it'll come for us all.

So she has to die, and we have to take what she has or we'll all die too. It's that simple."

A desperate breath left Zeke, as though all his arguments were drying up inside. A few yards away, Liana watched him.

"You can't stop us," Niall told him. "The guards from the camp are Sylphaen, and they'll be here any moment. Ren won't believe you, and Ina—"

Zeke's face darkened. "Don't you *touch* her."

"I won't. I'm not a monster. But Ina's life is at stake for as long as this creature lives and I need you to understand that. You're the one endangering Ina, not me. I'm only doing what's necessary to help our people survive." His hand tightened on my shoulder. "So get out of my way."

"No."

Niall made a frustrated noise and released his grip on my hair only to wrap his fingers around my neck. A hoarse gasp escaped me.

"I can hurt her, brother. Hurt her as much as it takes to get you to move. We need her alive for the ceremony, not unharmed."

The muscles in Zeke's jaw jumped. He glanced from me to Liana, and then tossed a quick look over his shoulder at whatever he felt in the distance.

Liana darted forward.

And I couldn't make a sound to warn him.

Her spikes swung at his chest. Niall shouted for her to stop.

Zeke twisted and ducked at the cry. Her arm arced through

the space where he'd been, and then he was behind her.

His spikes drove into her back.

Liana choked. Blood spread through the water between them.

Zeke's gaze rose to his brother, and I shivered at the look in his eyes. Shocked. Pained beyond words.

And strangely satisfied.

With a shaking hand, he reached over, unclipping the stone from Liana's belt before tugging his spikes from her back and letting her sink to the cave floor.

Niall's grip on me tightened. Zeke lifted the stone, his thumb hovering over it and ready to smash down.

"Let Chloe go," Zeke told him.

"You–"

"I said let Chloe go."

Niall didn't respond.

Zeke looked to me. The pain in his gaze strengthened.

I closed my eyes, bracing myself.

Niall's grip disappeared.

I gasped and spun to find him floating a few feet behind me, his hands up as he watched us both.

Quickly, I swam to Zeke. Reaching out, he caught the shackles as I came near. Swiftly, he undid the locks and then let the manacles drop to the ground.

"Our people are everywhere," Niall said. "Our mercenaries have gotten past every border, and they're watching for her too. You won't be able to keep her away from us forever."

Zeke wrapped his hand around mine. "Yes I will."

His eyes on his brother, Zeke pulled me with him as he retreated from the cave.

I could feel the guards in the distance the moment we were outside. I looked to Zeke.

His face was ashen, and in his eyes something had died. His gaze lingered on the shadows a moment more, while his brow twitched down with pain.

And then he glanced toward the guards.

"Come on," he said to me, his voice tight. "Fast as you can."

His hand gripping mine, we swam away from the hills and the cave.

The island was barely a nub of stone above the ocean's surface, and the boulders beneath it looked like shoreline that the sea had already managed to devour. A mile beyond it, a rugged coast waited, its rocky shores backed by towering evergreens for as far as my eyes could see. The waves rolled around me, the water the color of metal and tossed by winds that had dragged a blanket of gray across the sky. At Zeke's direction, we'd swam as hard as we could to reach this place, knowing that every moment we spent in the water just gave the Sylphaen or their mercenaries another chance to find us.

Though now that we were here, Zeke seemed to ignore it

all. He'd hardly said a word since we left the cave, barring the short instruction to head this way. He'd barely even looked up from the ocean floor.

With a worried glance to him below me, I dove back down and trailed him as he swam closer to one of the boulders. He pressed his fingers to various depressions on the stone, and then moved a hand to its side and briefly closed his eyes.

My brow furrowed in confusion. I cast a look over my shoulder, searching for the Sylphaen I knew would be coming.

Light caught the corner of my eye and I turned back. In a hollow on the boulder's face, the water seemed to shimmer and brighten, as though touched with a blue-white light.

"Work," Zeke muttered, not looking away from the rock, and I couldn't tell if he'd meant to say anything aloud. "Damned override, just work."

An image of the wall of a room resolved from the glistening water, revealing shelves and the edge of a fejeria-blocked window that looked familiar.

"What the–" someone cried. Ina appeared in the image. "Zeke? What–"

"Ina, just listen to me."

I could see fear come into her eyes at the words. At the harsh sound of them.

"Niall…" Zeke drew a rough breath. "Niall's a Sylphaen. It was all a setup. He's the one who killed Dad. Him and Liana. They did it to take control of Yvaria, to scare Ren, and to make it easier to get to Chloe. So you have to go to Ren.

You have to make him understand that. And you have to stay away from Niall. Whatever it takes. Stay away from him."

"Zeke, what—"

"Please."

She stared at him.

I looked back to the ocean. The Sylphaen would be here soon. The guards had been only a few minutes behind us this entire time. We had to go.

Zeke seemed to know it too.

"Just do it, okay?" he continued. "Please. I… I'll be home soon. I just have something I need to do first." He paused. "Love you, Ina."

He dropped his hand from the side of the boulder. The image wavered and vanished before Ina could say a word.

"What now?" I asked quietly.

For a moment, he didn't respond.

"Zeke?"

His brow twitched down, and his head turned toward me though he didn't meet my eyes.

"What?" he asked distantly.

I hesitated. "I asked what now?"

His gaze rose to mine for only a heartbeat before pain pulled it away again.

"Now we get you home."

He turned and swam for the coast.

An ache moved through me. I wanted to help him. I wanted to fix this somehow.

But short of what we were already doing, I couldn't think of a way.

Drawing a breath to keep me steady, I followed him toward the shore.

EPILOGUE

NOAH

The salty air moved around me and on the horizon, storm clouds formed. The tide swept in around my feet, stinging a bit at random scrapes from the car wreck earlier today.

My cousins were gone. Pretty soon, Baylie would be too. She'd already stayed longer than she'd planned, and after what had happened with my family, she was eager to return home. Meanwhile, Dad had taken care of the cops, though I probably wouldn't see my license again anytime soon. Maddox forgave me about the car, joking that he'd planned on giving it to me anyway. Diane claimed just to be glad I was alright, although it'd taken her several minutes of yelling to get around to admitting that point.

And now they all wanted to get back to normal.

Even if I wasn't sure what that looked like anymore.

Waves washed around my feet and then rushed out to sea.

It'd always felt better next to the ocean than anywhere else in the world. I'd never wanted to leave it, not for long anyway, and every time I had, I'd always been so happy to return home.

Until now.

The steps creaked behind me. I looked back to see Baylie coming down the stairs.

"Hey," she said quietly.

"Hey."

Her hand lingered on the banister, and her gaze dropped. With a bare toe, she nudged the sand. "I had a question."

I waited.

She glanced up at me. "You want a vacation?"

My brow furrowed.

Baylie tried for a smile. "I hear Kansas is... well, *calm*, this time of year."

I paused, taken back by the simple gesture. By the fact she wanted me around.

By how much of a relief it would be to get away from this place and the question of whether I'd ever see Chloe again.

Even if only for a while.

"Yeah," I replied, "that'd be nice."

Want to know what happens next?

Check out Return
Book three of the Awakened Fate series

Find out about new releases

Join my new release mailing list at skyemalone.com

Loved the book?

Awesome! Would you like to leave a review? Visit Amazon, Goodreads, or any other book-related site and tell people about it!

Other titles

The Awakened Fate series

The Children and the Blood trilogy (published under the name Megan Joel Peterson)

About the author

Skye Malone is a fantasy author, which means she spends most of her time not-quite-convinced that the things she imagines couldn't actually exist. Born and raised in central Illinois, she hopes someday to travel the world — though in the meantime she'll take any story that whisks her off to a place where the fantastic lives inside the everyday. She loves strong and passionate characters, complex villains, and satisfying endings that stay with you long after the book is done. An inveterate writer, she can't go a day without getting her hands on a keyboard, and can usually be found typing away while she listens to all the adventures unfolding in her head.

Connect with me

Website: www.skyemalone.com
Twitter: twitter.com/Skye_Malone
Facebook: facebook.com/authorskyemalone
Google Plus: plus.google.com/+SkyeMaloneAuthor

ACKNOWLEDGMENTS

Many thanks to everyone who supports this series.

To the wonderful people who've read these books: the Awakened Fate series wouldn't be what it is without you. Thank you so much for reading, for your support, and for your excitement about this story.

To Vicki Brown: thank you again for beta-reading, for your feedback, and for how much you've enjoyed this series.

To Tarra Peterson: thank you again for your thoughts and input, and for all your wonderful enthusiasm.

To my mother and sister, Mary Ann and Keri Offenstein: your support makes all the difference in the world. Thank you so much for all you've given me.

To my husband, Eugene: as always, this story wouldn't have happened without you. Thank you for everything.

Made in the USA
Charleston, SC
09 September 2016